Eye for an Eye

A Cobalt City and Justice-Vengeance Crossover

Written by Erik Scott de Bie

DefCon One Edition

ISBN: 1-948280-10-8 ISBN-978-1-948280-10-5

CONTENTS

PROLOGUE

ONE-EYED RAVEN

Half an hour ago

He awoke, his body instantly alert, to a flashing message on the computer screen across the room. He extricated himself from the two women in his bed, taking care not to wake them, and crossed to his desk. As the years passed, the likelihood of that particular alarm going off had grown smaller and smaller, but now it was time: the alarm indicated one particular intruder he had tried but failed to forget.

After so many years, she'd come back.

Hands trembling with uncertain expectation, he tapped the keys on his computer and scrutinized a live video feed. He knew her immediately, though he hadn't seen her in a decade. He knew the black leather, the hair, the familiar movements learned from their shared master. He recognized the silver claw she wore on her left hand, a weapon he had forged for her at the height of their passion. And most of all, he recognized the signature of her powers: her dark magic that sent unreasonable terror through his sentries and servants. Men of unshakable loyalty fled her, driven mad with fear.

It was her, as beautiful and terrible as ever. She'd come to face him.

He'd prepared for this moment for more than a decade, ever since he had seen her for the first time and realized what she could do. He had recognized her implicit threat immediately, even if no one else had. And though he'd spent years trying to deny it, to convince himself that she could hold the darkness at bay, part of him had always known that she represented a clear and present danger to the world of humanity.

He typed in a command: DAMPEN.EXE. His finger wavered over the enter key. He rubbed the lid of his dead left eye.

She'd come to die. This time, he would not disappoint her.

He pressed enter.

PART ONE

OLD ENEMIES

CHAPTER ONE

SOMEWHERE IN COLORADO ...

Considering how much blood kept leaking from the rip in her midsection, Lady Vengeance knew she was about to die.

Deep beneath the military complex, she limped down a red-lit hallway to the ear-shattering thunder of alarms, trying to see through pain-blurred eyes. She had to stop every so often just to catch her breath. Her claw scraped an unsteady path along the wall, whining as the titanium-vanadium alloy—the kind of metal used to build spacecraft engines—gouged the reinforced concrete. In the wake of the claw, dark blood traced a dripping line across the wall. It made a hell of a mess.

"Some superhero I am," she murmured. "Can't even die clean."

She reached out for her powers, but found only sucking emptiness. With a shiver, she recalled the bone-shredding agony of half an hour before, when she was hit with enough radiation to knock out an elephant. She hadn't even known power dampener tech existed, much less that it waited inside the bunker in Colorado. If she had, maybe she'd have rethought some things. Her life, for instance, and her forthcoming death.

What had convinced her coming to Valhalla was a good idea?

Now her own blood coated her silvery claw and plastered her black leather outfit to her shivering frame. She still fit into the tights, despite putting on a few pounds around 40, though she went for full pants these days rather than that ridiculous skirt thingy, and definitely not the fishnets. She tried to work out, though now that time felt like a waste, since she was going to die anyway.

She kept thinking about how she should have eaten more totchos.

Shuffling step after shuffling step smeared her blood across the cold marble hallway. Wheezing, Lady Vengeance paused at an intersection and cast a weary glance both ways. It looked as though she had a moment to rest. She should have sat, if only to die peacefully, but she stayed standing.

"Come on," she said. "Come on, soldier—"

She might have been eviscerated, power-drained, and absolutely, positively *fucked*, but if she stopped, she would be dead, too.

Her pursuer, after all, would never give up.

Vivienne only meant to hold herself up against the wall with one hand, but naturally she leaned her whole body against it. The floor looked so, *so* comfortable.

"Come on," she whispered. "Don't—ok. Just a minute. That's it. Just—"

Vivienne sank down the wall, leaving a thick smear of red and black blood down the sterile stone wall. Her bloody lips split open and she tried to laugh, which came out more as a cough.

"At least," Vivienne said. "At least I'm going to mess up your little secret research installation, you bird-faced fuck."

One had to take pleasure in the little things.

It wasn't entirely her fault. Even if she had powers of healing or teleportation or just superhuman toughness—which she didn't—none of them would function after the dampener hit. The liquor was long gone, swallowed up in a wave of adrenaline, and even the diazepam she'd knocked back was starting to fade. The more blood she lost, the harder it became to move. She had to find a med lab and hope ...

From somewhere behind her, she heard metal pound against metal—fists breaking open a security door she'd managed to close. It had delayed the avenging vigilante, but to what end? She didn't have an escape route in mind.

"No escape this time," she murmured. "Yay, me."

The pounding increased in volume, and finally she heard metal scream to the breaking point. Back down the hall, a huge iron blast door went tumbling into the opposite wall with a roar to rival a crashing jet. Breathing hard and fighting to stay awake, Lady

Vengeance watched the devastation in the middle of a shrinking world.

"Get up," she said. "Up—"

A man stepped through the fire and smoke, girded in black metal and leather. A robotic exoskeleton reinforced his torso and limbs, and blades bristled from his hands and cape. One of those had been the weapon that had cut open Lady Vengeance's middle, and her blood still dripped from it onto the floor. He turned toward her, but not with a man's face—rather, he wore the scythe-like beak of a carrion bird. A single bright red eye gleamed from the left side of his mask.

The Raven.

"Not yet," she said. "Not dead yet."

Seeing him gave her the rush of adrenaline she needed to push herself to her feet. Lady Vengeance stumbled down the hallway, not sure where she was going.

The Raven followed, taking his time. They both knew she could not escape.

As Lady Vengeance limped around a corner, a door swished open. She looked up, blearily, and her heart lurched. The red cross on the window marked this as an emergency medical station. She staggered in, pressed herself back against the wall just inside the door, and hit the "lock" button. The door shut and gave an angry beep.

Hollow metallic footsteps drew closer and closer, and a shadow passed over the window. The Raven paused, and Lady Vengeance could see the glow from his red eye peering into the medical bay. The door whined, rejecting his entry after she'd activated the emergency lock. Maybe he'd interpret that as meaning the door had been locked before, and she hadn't been able to get in. If he could track her with his radar, though, she was fucked.

Then, after what seemed like forever, he moved on. Blood pounding in her ears, Lady Vengeance listened to his footsteps move away, and finally dared to breathe out.

She rummaged through the sparse med bay, which was equipped with an emergency wash station, a foldable stretcher, and a first aid kit. It was hard to open the kit with her shaking claw, but she had to use her other hand to keep her insides from becoming her outsides. Inside, she found bandages, antiseptic, and, best of all, two little syringes with a white label. Reverex.

"I take back everything I ever said about you, Raven," she murmured. "Well, except all the bad stuff."

She bandaged herself up as best she could, then stuck the syringe in her middle. Immediately, she felt a little better, or maybe that was just hope. In her addled state, she thought she could feel the minds of all those nanobots, all with their little hopes and fears, going to work stitching her back together. Which was of course ridiculous—her powers were dampened, and she never absorbed anything from robots anyway.

This was only a temporary fix. If the Raven got close, he could probably deactivate them with his armor. Not much of a fight when he could kill her with the push of a button. "Son of a bitch," she murmured. "Never could fight fair."

The door beeped angrily behind her. Lady Vengeance whirled to see the Raven's face in the window of the med bay—the only exit. She was trapped.

A second time, the Raven tried to disable the security, but the system rejected him. His predecessor had built these lower levels, after all, and this Raven apparently wasn't an admin on these systems. Instead, metal shrieked against metal as the Raven brought up one of his wings to slash across the door. Lady Vengeance flinched at the awful sound. Over and over, the Raven cut at the door. With his diamond-sharp feathers, he'd be through in a minute. The whole time, he kept his red eye fixed on her.

Lady Vengeance stared back, panting, and reached out for fear to empower herself. Power whispered at the edge of her consciousness—faint and muddied from the dampener, but there, barely controlled. She couldn't fight the Raven, but maybe she could get past him. She tasted the Raven's emotions—mostly rage, but also a little sweet, sweet fear. Was he afraid she would escape? Regardless, this was her chance.

Vivienne, a voice whispered—one she recognized entirely too well.

"Shut up," she murmured. It would be a bad, bad thing to listen to that voice.

The Raven burst through the door, and she rushed him. She channeled all the fear she could absorb and jabbed her clawed hand at his chest. The barbs bit into his power armor, doing negligible damage, but it was the fear that was important. She poured it all on him, lashing at his mind with the terror she had absorbed. The

Raven's body jerked upright, and he staggered back against the far wall.

Finish him, the voice whispered.

"Fuck off," she said.

Still, her powers were acting up, barely under her control, and Lady Vengeance didn't wait around. She ran on, limping and trying not to vomit. The dusty corridors down here felt unused, which reassured her. Escape was barely even on her mind anymore—it was just her body trying to get away from certain death.

Unfortunately, the hallway ended in a sealed laboratory door with a palm reader security system. It looked old, as though the Raven hadn't updated it since the days of Supergroup. She pressed a shaking hand to the palm reader, but it returned a red "ACCESS DENIED" message. Blood smeared across the LED screen as she shifted her hand, but no luck. Of course the Raven would have disabled her security clearance, but she didn't recognize this system. What was in this lab?

She heard metallic footsteps down the hall behind her. She was out of time.

His fear filled Lady Vengeance, and she turned it into strength. She raked her unbreakable claw through the door seal, and it popped open. Propped against an inside wall was a metal hoop attached to dusty machinery. On the walls were posted yellow maps, each of them tagged with multiple yellow stickies marked with coordinates.

She knew what this was, now: matter transference tech. The second Raven—her current pursuer's mentor—had discontinued the project after the accident that cost him the mantle. He'd never told anyone where the tech was located, though—could his last experiment still be active?

Lady Vengeance stumbled up to the computer console, which whirred on as she entered. It blinked a request for coordinates. She punched in numbers she thought were on the East Coast but didn't much care. Anywhere but Colorado was good. Silvery light spread in the middle of the teleportation hoop, and she saw a bleary room full of people.

The door shattered open, and the Raven strode through the twisting metal. He raised his arm launcher toward her, and it was now or never.

"Too slow!" She slashed her claw through the computers, then fell into the circle, her good hand raised in a one-finger salute.

~

The Raven watched his quarry vanish into the matter-transference wormhole, which wavered, destabilized. She'd shredded the computer, so the portal was about to close. He cursed himself inwardly for hesitating to shoot her. She'd surprised him by fighting off the effects of the damper. Probably her powers were coming back wild, though, which was to his advantage. He focused on the blinking red coordinates she'd put in on the read-out attached to the transference hoop: Cobalt City.

They hardly knew what was about to hit them.

He activated his comm. "H. Departing for Cobalt City. Track me."

"S-72 ready to deploy in five minutes," she said in his earpiece.

"Won't need it," he replied in his gravelly voice, then hung up.

As the Raven considered the failing portal, he opened his mask and rubbed at his empty eye socket. Thin scars cut across his brow and down his cheek where a familiar silver claw had gouged the eye out.

"This isn't over," the Raven said, and stepped through.

CHAPTER TWO

THE OUT-OF-TOWNERS

"Do we *have* to?" Chuck rolled her eyes.

"Yes, we do!" Jaccob Stevens replied with the brilliant, ingratiating smile that had always worked on his children—until they hit their teens, anyway. "Your mother has that benefit dinner to go to tonight, so you're stuck with me. But it'll be fun! Promise! I'll buy you an ice cream."

"An ice cream, Dad? Really?"

"Unless you want a frozen yogurt."

Chuck rolled her eyes. "I'm fifteen, Dad."

"Is that a no?"

"Fine." Chuck crossed her arms and stared out the window. "If it's strawberry."

Jaccob pulled the SUV into the towering Cobalt City Skymall. Eight parking floors supported four shopping towers, interconnected by an elaborate series of skywalks. Every store had a great view of the surrounding city. It was one of Cobalt City's most modern buildings, built with a generous grant from Jaccob's own Starcom Industries. With his superhero days becoming less and less frequent over the years, Jaccob had recently turned his fortune to construction, rather than destruction. Which was better for his image, if somewhat less fun.

As Stardust, Cobalt City's preeminent superhero and symbol of Starcom, Jaccob had broken ground on the site himself with his star-blasters two years ago, then only a few months ago parted the ribbon for the Skymall's grand opening with the much less impressive laser cutter. (This he had done at the Board of Directors' request, owing to the regrettable star-blaster ground-breaking incident two years ago.)

Those had been the days. He'd hardly had a reason to put on his armor for years, and he wasn't getting any younger.

They hit the clothing stores first. Chuck shunned the high-end boutiques in favor of a dark, cramped store that blared rock music. No stranger to teenage behavior, Jaccob hung back and tried to look like he didn't know her.

Jaccob had been Chuck's fifth choice as a mall chaperone. She wanted first to go alone, then with her mother, or her brother Mike, or possibly alone again. As a teenager, this attitude was to be expected, as was her dark taste in clothes.

"Interesting how fashion is cyclical," Jaccob said when she came out of the store with two black plastic bags. "Goth was the look when I was young, too."

"It's not a look," Chuck said. "I'm just wearing my feelings on the outside."

"Uh huh." His phone buzzed. "Hang on a second."

He rolled up his sleeve to check his HUD, but the call hadn't come through there. Huh. He had to pick up his phone and check the read-out, which listed a phone number: an old school page. "That's funny—"

"Dad, you're doing that thing again," Chuck said.

"What thing?" Jaccob asked.

"That thing where you have to check every single doohickey you carry around."

"I am not." Jaccob took his hand out of his coat pocket, where he'd been reaching to check his police scanner or music player (he hadn't decided which to use first). He whipped out his secret change-the-subject technique: "How about shoes next?"

Predictably, Chuck brightened. As gothy as her preferences in clothing might run, she had an abiding passion for shoes. She made it five steps before she turned around. "You're trying to get rid of me, aren't you?"

"Of course not," Jaccob lied.

"No, it's cool—I just wanted to make sure."

"Do you have your personal Jaccobean particle forcefield projector?"

Chuck rubbed her wristwatch and groaned. "Yes, Dad."

"Meet me back here in ten minutes."

She beat tracks, the way only a newly liberated teen can.

"Huh." Jaccob felt vaguely tricked—as though Chuck had taken the upper hand, somehow. Then the page blew up his phone again, and he forgot all about it. He fed the number into his HUD to start a trace.

Now he recognized the number: a Protectorate distress call. Even after the group broke up, he hadn't disabled all the old secret numbers, and call forwarding must be active. Maybe he'd forgotten, or maybe he'd subconsciously held out hope that one day, one of those numbers would get a ping again. Regardless, someone needed help—someone in the Skymall, in fact.

He hurried back to the parking garage, filled with the sort of dizzy excitement he hadn't experienced since the Charger had zoomed into town and started half the cars fighting each other in the streets. Maybe even since he'd knocked a fiery Ferris Wheel out of the sky the day that the Golden Apple Carnival had almost eaten Cobalt City.

Duty had (literally) called, and Stardust had a mission!

He took the elevator to P4 and raced toward his SUV, inputting commands into his HUD as he went. The SUV beeped open and he threw himself into the driver's seat. He hit "execute" on his HUD, and mechanisms started pulling the vehicle apart. The top half of the car split off and molded itself to fit his torso and shoulders, and parts of the engine reached over to attach themselves to his arms. His Starbands clasped around his wrists, and the car attached most of the radio to his head as his helmet.

In a matter of seconds, Jaccob Stevens wore his Stardust armor, and his SUV had become a jeep.

Stardust leaped into the air and flew out of the parking structure, one eye on his radar and the other on the mall. He circled, isolated the source of the distress call—a cell phone on the third floor—and locked on. He flew toward it, one hand pointing the way. Cobalt City's mightiest, not-quite-retired, flashiest hero should make an entrance.

He hadn't done this in a while, though, so when he erred on the side of speed, he came in a little bit hot.

The reinforced wall of Elizabeth's Secret—which Stardust insisted was named after his goddess of a wife—exploded as he missed the window. The armored superhero tumbled in amidst a cascade of drywall, electrical wire, and ladies' undergarments. When he recovered, he came face to face with a wild-eyed, pale woman dressed all in black leaning heavily on a bin of panties and bras marked "50% Off."

"Fuck," she said. "This doesn't look like Bora Bora."

Blood and sweat plastered her raven hair to her head, and her midsection looked like hamburger. She held a cellphone and a bloodstained business card in one white-knuckled hand, while she menaced her fellow customers with some kind of silver-metal claw on the other. Stardust stepped toward her, and she frowned at him.

"Hello!" Stardust boomed through his voice enhancers, making her wince.

"Great, another armored tech hero," she said in a ragged voice. "Didn't I just leave this noise?"

Mall security was on the scene, though they looked deathly terrified. Stardust didn't see anything intimidating about the woman, other than maybe the claw. She was clearly of the costume set, which gave him pause, but she had no wings or wielded any obvious dangerous gizmos. She was petite, about forty, attractive, and obviously very hurt. She looked more like she needed serious help than a good tasing.

"Welcome to Cobalt City!" he said. "You look like you need medical attention."

"A little bit." The woman turned her attention on him, and while she seemed wary, she didn't look intimidated in the least. She showed him the crumpled business card. "Are you with the Protectorate? This kid Castile gave me this card for emergencies."

Stardust's eyes widened. "The Huntsman? You—" He shook his head. "I'm Stardust—a *former* member of the Protectorate. Come with me. We'll sort this all out."

"Yeah, *that* seems likely." Her eyes seemed suddenly very dark. "Oh, fuck me."

Stardust wasn't sure what wasn't likely—that she'd come with him or that all this would work out—and he had no idea what that last part meant. But he was done trying to placate her. Whoever she was, this woman obviously had a history with the Protectorate, and if she didn't get to a doctor soon, she would pass out or worse.

He took a step forward. "Now look—"

"Sorry in advance," she said as darkness gathered around her. Her eyes were jet-black, like pools of crude oil. "I'm not doing this on purpose."

Suddenly, a crippling terror seized his limbs and brain. Past the woman, he saw his daughter Chuck, who had come to check out the disturbance at Elizabeth's Secret. She stepped forward as though to say something, but a faceless man in a black suit pressed a kerchief over her mouth, seized her, and hauled her off.

"Chuck!" he shouted and shot off in that direction. His heart raced, and he felt like he was moving through mud. He forgot all about the woman in black.

The man was fast—dragging Chuck kicking and struggling all the way down the corridor toward the elevators—but Stardust's booster rockets were faster. He slammed into the man with a flying tackle that would have taken out the toughest linebacker. As expected, the man offered little resistance, but Stardust hadn't calculated that he'd feel like *nothing*. He plowed right through the kidnapper and crashed into the wall, shattering the drywall and cratering the brick beneath. Stardust fell to the floor and shook his head.

"Ok," he said. "What just happened?

"*Dad*," Chuck said. "You're embarrassing me."

Stardust looked around at the mall-goers gawking at him. His daughter stood over him, two bags of shoes in her hands. Her would-be kidnapper was nowhere to be seen, as though he'd never been there at all. And even if he had, how had he penetrated Chuck's forcefield to grab her anyway? He checked his HUD scanner, and found no heat outline that matched the man he'd seen. An illusion?

"Man," he murmured. "I *hate* magic."

The woman in black was gone, but he thought his radar could track her energy signature or at least the trail of blood. She was confused, wounded, and potentially very dangerous. Leaving her to run amok was not an option, but he had something to do first.

"Chuck," he said. "I need to go find that woman, but you have to get home."

She brightened. "Does this mean I get the car?"

He held out his arms to carry her.

Chuck stuck out her tongue. "Ugh! Lame!"

~

Seconds later, the Raven strode out of the same portal into the middle of Elizabeth's Secret. Lady Vengeance's uncontrolled fear powers had mostly emptied the store, but people had started to trickle back in. The Raven's sudden appearance—a black-chrome phantom with a sharp beak and one burning red eye—out of what looked like thin air made them shriek and flee.

Security was still on the scene, and they fumbled for their tasers. "Freeze!"

The Raven ignored them and focused instead on his sensors. Lady Vengeance had been here, all right, and used her powers. Sure enough, after the dampener, they were coming back uncontrolled, making her a significant danger to bystanders. Or he was too late, and she'd already lost her mind and soul. Either way, he had to stop her.

He detected echoes of Vivienne Cain's unique DNA—specifically, a bloody trail—but his tech wasn't sophisticated enough to pick her out of a city of millions. He could scan people one-by-one, but that would take too long. Unfortunately for her, he'd registered the lingering energy signature of the matter-transference event and could at least initially track her that way. She seemed to be flying? That wasn't in her power set.

"H-hands up!" Four security guards.

The Raven didn't have time for this, particularly if he had to track Lady Vengeance on foot.

He targeted one taser, and a razor shot from his cloak to knock it aside, so that it shocked a second guard. Even as they stared, shocked, the Raven rushed forward into the confused group. Within three seconds, the four rent-a-cops slumped unconscious at his feet. He checked his HUD, which was picking up the powerful energy signature he'd tracked earlier. A tech hero was out and about, probably hunting Lady Vengeance now.

Perhaps this would be easier than the Raven had expected.

CHAPTER THREE

THAT SPECIAL LADY

After flying his daughter back up to the penthouse of Starcom Tower, Stardust headed right back out to find the woman who had teleported into the bargain bin at Elizabeth's Secret and was leaving a trail of blood and terror across Cobalt City.

Adventure!

As he flew past the construction of the other tower at Starcom plaza—which was coming along pretty well, if he was any judge, which he wasn't—his tech picked up social media reports of people going hysterical in the streets from the Skymall to Lafayette Park. They would stagger for a moment, then freak out and scream about the sky falling, or monsters appearing, or something like that, which no one else could see. Many of the comments mentioned a strange woman in black who staggered into or otherwise interacted with victims shortly before their apparent insanity would strike. Exactly what had happened to Stardust in the Skymall.

"Fear magic—man, I *hate* magic," he murmured. "Computer, run a check on known contacts of Marcus Castile, a.k.a. the Huntsman. Cross-reference superhuman abilities, power-set magic, fear-based."

"Processing," said the sexy computer voice. "Found reference to superheroine Lady Vengeance, real name Vivienne Cain, in 2005 report filed by Marcus Castile, sub-title: 'Vengeance on the Layover.'"

"Clever," he said.

"As you indicate, Jaccob."

"Call me Stardust when I'm in the armor. On screen, 30 percent opacity."

As he circled Lafayette Park, he scanned through the Huntsman's report. Vivienne Cain's physical description matched the woman he'd seen in the mall: middle-aged, black hair and pale skin, and (as Huntsman euphemistically put it) "well-built." This "Lady Vengeance" was an empath who could absorb a person's fearful emotions. So empowered, she could shape the energy into quasi-solid objects, scramble a victim's mind with illusions, or transform herself into an incarnation of her victim's worst fear.

"Cuddly," Stardust said. "Known weaknesses, Computer?"

"Frequent struggles with alcoholism and ... Definitional query: What does 'a thing for married men' indicate?"

Stardust shook his head. "Liz is gonna *kill* me."

His radar picked up Lady Vengeance in a public restroom near the north end of the park. A dozen or so people gathered around the squat building, writhing on the ground and trying to escape phantoms only they could see. He landed and turned his speakers on high. "Never fear, citizens. I, Stardust, am here to save the day!"

A whole visiting party of tourists stampeded past, exclaiming something about a giant monster and pointing back the way they'd come.

"Huh." If Lady Vengeance was trying to escape, it seemed pretty careless of her to make such a scene. Maybe her powers were going haywire?

He turned his broadcaster toward the restroom. "Welcome to Cobalt City! My name is Jaccob Stevens—Stardust—licensed hero and appointed guardian of Cobalt City. You're Vivienne Cain, a.k.a. Lady Vengeance, right? Can I help you in some way?"

There was no movement inside the restroom. Sirens rang out distantly.

"Police are on their way, but I think we can sort this out peacefully. How 'bout it?"

No response.

"Excuse me? Ms. Femme Fatale? I know you're in there. And I couldn't help but notice you're in dire need of medical attention. So come out, and let's get you fixed up."

Stardust fidgeted, but there was no sign of Lady Vengeance.

"Ok, I'm giving you three seconds. Three ... two ... one?"

Still, no response.

"Have it your way." He did the targeting calculations, charged up his blasters to humming with Jaccobean particles, and swept his hands up and across. Two Starbolts blasted the front half of the park restroom into a storm of kindling and ash. Standing in front of a now-bared sink and broken mirror in the center of the mess, Lady Vengeance recoiled to shield her face, then looked at him tiredly. She'd been in the middle of changing the bandages on her midsection with blood-soaked hands.

"You're being a tool, Shiny," she said. "Can't a girl get a little privacy?"

"Vivienne Cain, I presume? I'm Stardust."

"Call me V." She nodded. "What if I'd been on the pot, Sparkle-motion? Huh?"

"It's *Stardust.*" He drew up to his full height. "Lady Vengeance, you represent a clear and present danger to Cobalt City, and—"

"Woah there, Mr. Gratuitous Property Destruction—*I'm* a danger to the city?" She gestured around at the destroyed public restroom. "What do you call this?"

"Collateral damage in pursuit of a potentially dangerous criminal. Oh, you're under arrest, by the way, before this gets any worse."

"Worse?" Lady Vengeance looked amused. "Oh, you've got no idea."

She raised her silver claw, which was smeared with blood. Its diamond tips sparkled. Unease flickered in Stardust's stomach, but he fought it down.

"Aren't you hurt?" he asked. "That *is* your blood, right?"

"I got better," she said.

Stardust ran a quick diagnostic scan, and sure enough, her tissue was being repaired even as he scanned her. She had lithium and other chemicals in her system—possible drug use—and her blood alcohol was a little high. He also detected foreign material in her bloodstream—something that seemed almost alive.

"Nanobots?" he asked, so fascinated he almost forgot about the standoff. "That's years ahead of my tech. Where'd you get it?"

"Stole it." Lady Vengeance shrugged. "Let's just get on with it. Hit me with your best shot."

Stardust obliged with a Starbolt powerful enough to stun her, but somehow, she dodged aside like an Olympic gymnast. It was almost like magic. Maybe he'd been worried about hurting her, or else the Computer had messed up the calculations. The queasiness in his stomach rose to full-on nausea, and he found his hands were starting to shake with anxiety.

"Computer, what's happening?" he asked. "Computer?"

No response.

"Hey, Shiny!" Lady Vengeance called.

A silvery claw raked across his faceplate, scratching the glass and snapping his head back. Stardust staggered and swung wildly but hit nothing. Why was his forcefield down? His HUD said it was up, but only his armor seemed to be stopping her claw.

She kept moving, so that every time he tried to lock on, she would vanish like a ghost before his computer could respond. He couldn't get a clear shot, not to mention the scratches blurred his vision.

"Sorry about the queasy," Lady Vengeance said. "I was power-drained earlier. My powers are coming back, though. Good for me—bad for you."

Stardust shook himself. "I'm not afraid of you."

"No, but you're afraid of *something*, and that's enough for me."

Lady Vengeance circled Stardust and darted in to rake at him from unexpected angles, then retreated before he could counter. He felt like a deer trying to escape a wolf. His agitation grew, and Stardust tried to calm himself down. It was all in his head—the more afraid she made him, the more powerful she became. She was just an empath—wounded and barely armed—and he was *Stardust*, dammit.

"I can feel you fighting me, Shiny," Lady Vengeance said. "Admirable, but you might as well give up now. Take it easy on both of us."

She was right. He'd figure this out, but by the time he did, she'd have absorbed too much of his fear and it would be too late. He felt helpless, just as he had in the Skymall when he thought someone was kidnapping Chuck.

Chuck!

At the memory, anger rose up and drowned Stardust's fear. He couldn't seem to access his targeting computer—probably, her powers were screwing with his perceptions—but he sure as hell could fire *manually*.

Stardust diverted power to his blasters and fired in a 360-degree arc, drawing a circle of concussive force. The remaining half of the restroom blew apart, pulverized by his blast, while trees flinched and the earth churned under his feet. Most rewarding was Lady Vengeance's surprised "unf," followed by the sound of a body hitting pavement. Instantly, the woman's hold on Stardust's emotions disintegrated, and he felt like himself again. He could see and think straight.

"Are you all right, Stardust?" asked the Computer. "Repeat command?"

All the mechanisms in his armor were blinking at full power. Lady Vengeance hadn't shut them down—she'd just fooled him with that illusion. It made sense, because he feared his technology failing him when it counted. *Magic.* Ugh.

"Stardust?" The Computer sounded worried.

"Nothing," he said. "I'm good. We're good."

Good thing he'd set the blast to stun. In his panic, he might have really hurt her.

Lady Vengeance lay groaning on the sidewalk a few yards away, just at the edge of the circle, where the grass stood up from flat. Blood ran from her nose, but she looked otherwise unhurt. Her nanobots seemed to have healed her almost entirely.

"Nice," she said as he stood over her. "Didn't expect that."

"You knew," he said. "How to move—how to mess up my computer."

Her eyes rolled. "Luck."

"Didn't seem like luck." Stardust considered. "The nanobots, this power dampener you mentioned—you've fought a techsavant before, and recently. Who?"

Lady Vengeance smiled. "Guess you better arrest me, Shiny. Heh."

Stardust scooped her up and powered up his boot jets. She giggled. "What's so funny?"

"You'll see," she said. "The Raven is coming—and that's going to *suck*."

"The Raven? Is he the tech hero who's after you?"

"He's close. God, I need ... drink—" Lady Vengeance fainted.

Stardust couldn't help a little thrill of suspicion, so he did a scan of the surrounding area. He shifted through the spectra of his instruments, from infrared to ultraviolet and beyond. He picked up nothing, except a little static on the Jaccobean spectrum (a wavelength only detectable by the Stardust particles).

"She's messing with me." Stardust cradled Lady Vengeance close and took off. "Computer, autopilot to police headquarters."

~

The Raven lurked in the shadows of a nearby oak tree, his stealth setting on max. Even so, he knew Stardust had almost detected him, which was impressive.

Of course the Raven had files on Stardust—it wasn't like the man kept a low profile. Jaccob Stevens, Chief Operating Officer in charge of Research and Development at Starcom Industries, an internationally recognized company with defense and commercial interests beyond U.S. borders. He'd consistently blocked their influx into Valhalla, of course, and he'd never met Stevens face-to-face. Now that he had, he found he respected the man more than he thought he would.

After all, Stardust's tech wasn't entirely insufficient.

He clicked on his comm and called his espionage specialist. "M."

"*Capitán!*" the reply came, almost instantly. "We were worried! You just dis—"

"Run a report on Starcom," he said, right over her concerned voice. "Tech, finances, market share. Focus on Jaccob Stevens, CEO, a.k.a. Stardust."

M was silent for a moment, then crackled: "Affirmative."

The Raven nodded. "H."

"*¿Si, capitán?*" said his tech specialist.

The Raven paused, considering. Then: "Nothing. Stand by."

He followed along on the ground, as flying would put him immediately on Stardust's radar, stealth tech or no.

He'd been about to request reinforcements, but he would do recon before he went to war with Jaccob Stevens and Stardust. Perhaps the man could be reasoned with, or perhaps he would simply be careless and give the Raven a free second.

More than enough time to shoot Lady Vengeance in the head.

CHAPTER FOUR

RUMBLE DOWNTOWN

"Incoming call from Liz, mobile," the Computer said.

"OK. Hang on—" Stardust alighted on the old Bailey, because his wife had always told him not to face-chat and fly.

A tiny holographic image appeared on his pop-up screen. "Hi, honey." Elizabeth Stevens looked down at the blood-covered woman in Stardust's arms. "Who's that?"

"Not entirely sure, actually," he said. "You're not jealous, are you?"

Liz gave him a cool look, one eyebrow raised. "No, honey, I just know you. You're going off on one of your half-cocked, spontaneous adventures, aren't you?"

"Nope," Stardust said. "Promise. I'm 100% cocked. Er."

Her eyebrow rose higher.

"Totally under control," he said. "I just have to run this goth-dressing, dimension-hopping, fear-inducing super-villain down to the police station, and I'll be home in time for Mike's soccer game." He paused. "Though ... well, maybe until I get this super-villain thing done, you and the kids had better go up to the cabin for a few days. I might be onto something big and potentially dangerous."

"Everything you do is big and potentially dangerous." Liz returned a long-patient sigh. "I have some things to do in the city, but after that, ok. I could use a few days away anyway. Remember the dry cleaning, and try not to get repulsor burns on it this time?"

"That's never, cvcr happened. Except the last couple times. Four, tops."

Liz disappeared into a message that said "call ended."

The conversation left Stardust vaguely uneasy. He loved talking to his wife, true, but whenever he took one of her calls in the armor, he felt like she gave him a gently castigating look. He felt a little like a boy caught in his mom's headlights with a toy he wasn't supposed to play with. And this videochat proved no exception.

Maybe he was just tired.

Lady Vengeance stirred. "Who was that?"

"My wife, actually," Stardust said.

"You're married? Like, to a woman?"

"You sound surprised."

"Sorry, I saw the skin-tight blue power suit and just assumed."

Stardust couldn't imagine what she meant. He cleared his throat. "You married?"

"God, no," she said. "Must be tough, being a family man and a superhero, being tied down and unable to go jetting off whenever. She sounds gorgeous, though."

"Yes, yes she is. Unfortunately, they don't make 'em that gorgeous downtown."

"OK, Cheesedust." Vivienne coughed raggedly. "You're seriously taking me to the police? Oh yeah, that's gonna go *great*."

"What do you mean? Is this about that Raven person who's following you?"

"*The* Raven," Vivienne corrected. "And when you meet him, whatever you do, don't say 'nevermore.' He hates that." She sounded casual, but her eyes were afraid.

"You can relax," he said. "You're safe. I'm taking you to the police."

"It won't matter," she said. "And it's not true, you know. What you told your wife."

"What wasn't?"

"I'm not a super-villain." Her eyes glazed. "The rest, ok, but not that."

She put her fingers up to his face, but there was no magic there. Instead, she just smeared some half-congealed blood on his already scratched faceplate. She slipped back into half-consciousness before he could ask for an explanation.

Stardust considered what she'd said, coupled with Liz's concerns. He hadn't realized he was on a spontaneous adventure, but now that she said the words, they fit. He hadn't taken the armor out for more than the occasional joyride and/or mugging in years. He had to admit, there was something exciting about being back in the saddle, shirking his responsibilities once in a while.

Stardust fired up the boot jets and took off for the police station.

~

His stealth tech had functioned more than adequately so far during the chase, so the Raven took to the rooftops to follow them. Stardust's loud boot-jets were about as far from subtle as one could get, but they certainly gave him some speed. Fortunately, the Raven had kept in top physical condition since he was nine years old, and his suit's cybernetic enhancements kept him in the chase. He leaped from rooftop to rooftop, sometimes perching on chimneys and hiding as needed.

Stardust seemed focused on his prisoner, but where was he taking her?

The Cobalt City police station appeared, and Stardust made a beeline for it. The Raven scowled. If Lady Vengeance were safely arrested, there was no way he could do what must be done, for the sake of the world.

The Raven switched to combat mode.

~

This time, Stardust took great care to land softly at the entrance of the station. In his experience, the cops tended to react poorly when he crashed through their lobby. It had only been the one time, but he kept the article framed in his office as a constant reminder to go easy on buildings and other inanimate objects.

Stardust popped his helmet open to address the bewildered receptionist. "Greetings," he said. "Licensed superhero Stardust here. I've apprehended the woman behind the recent public disturbances. Do you accept a transfer of custody?"

Cautiously, two policemen came out from behind the security door and cuffed the woozy Lady Vengeance. She smiled and shook her head, murmuring something about the futility of it all. Stardust didn't recognize this new generation of cops. The ones he'd known well back in the day had all retired after long service or resigned, citing psychological distress not unconnected to Stardust himself.

"She's an empath, so exercise extreme caution," he said. "I recommend a sedative of some kind. She's got active lithium in her system—possibly to treat bipolar disorder or depression. Be careful you don't mix chemicals."

They read Lady Vengeance her rights, then led her back into the station. As she went, she cast Jaccob a rueful smile. "See ya never, handsome," she said.

He couldn't help a little shiver at the finality of her words, or was it the flirtation? He couldn't deny that she was attractive, even covered with blood and in handcuffs, but Stardust had never so much as entertained thoughts of disloyalty to his bombshell wife and their wonderful kids. Something was disconcerting about Lady Vengeance, and it wasn't just her fear powers.

"Do you need anything else?" Stardust asked the man at the desk. "I've got a statement prepared. I took the liberty of recording it on the flight over."

"I think we have enough to investigate—hey! You!"

At first Stardust was startled, but he realized the cop was looking past him toward the doors. He turned, just in time to catch some kind of disruptor blast to the chest that shut off every electronic system in his suit. An electromagnetic pulse?

Then another object struck him: two electrodes that ...

His whole body suddenly went taut and he spasmed uncontrollably, then hit the ground. His armor had partly protected him from the shock, but *damn*, that had hurt.

"C-c-computer," he said. "Re-re-reboot—"

The Jaccobean particle technology in his Starbands stirred, and power started to flow back into the suit.

"Estimated time to reboot," said the Computer cheerily. "Forty seconds."

"Faster?" Stardust asked.

"I apologize, Stardust," she said. "Thirty-five seconds."

A man—or maybe it was a machine—stepped over him: a black statue of scored metal and leather, with a lightly clicking cape of metal trailing from his shoulders. He turned his bird-like helmet down toward Stardust for a moment, weighing him with a single piercing red eye on the left side of the mask. He looked like a carrion bird of some kind, like a crow—or a raven.

The Raven is coming, Lady Vengeance had said. *And that's going to suck.*

"You're him, aren't you?" Stardust said. "The technosavant she was talking about. What do you want?"

The Raven offered no response, but instead swept up his cloak like wings. A razor shard of metal detached from the cloak and shattered the bullet-proof glass over the front desk. The cop dove for cover, and the Raven leaped up to perch on the desk. Then he lunged through.

"Fifteen seconds to reboot," said the Computer.

"Come on!" Stardust shouted.

"You should relax, Jaccob," she said. "Ten seconds. Would you like a massage?"

"It's Stardust, and *no*! Turn the systems back on!"

"Yes, Stardust. Five seconds."

Cries of alarm rose deeper in the station. "I really need to speed up that reboot."

His armor whirred to life. "All systems active," said the Computer. "Are you sure you don't want a massage?"

"Full power."

Stardust rose with a groan of gyros, fired up his jets, and shot after the Raven.

~

Lady Vengeance sensed the Raven even before he burst through the front wall, before the first cry of alarm went up, and even before he entered the police station.

She could tell he was there because all of a sudden, she felt ill, and two seconds later, her stomach felt like someone had stabbed her.

"What's wrong?" said one of the cops—a good-looking guy with blond hair who was actively trying not to check her out.

"Shit." Blood filled Lady Vengeance's mouth and she spat it onto the floor.

"Jesus," said the cop. "Hey, are you all right? Call an ambulance!"

The Raven was here, and he had deactivated his Reverex nanobots. If she hadn't bandaged herself, her guts would be squishing onto the floor just then.

"He's coming," she managed, trying vainly to shove the cop aside.

As if on cue, the front desk window shattered, and the Raven leaped onto it, where he crouched like a hunting raptor. His red eye found her with laser-like focus.

Then every cop in the place turned a gun or a taser on the Raven, and chaos erupted. Bullets and electrodes flew everywhere, but the Raven shrugged them all off and stalked implacably toward his prey, throwing over desks and computers with abandon. The blond cop stood protectively over the choking Lady Vengeance, gun shaking in both hands, but the Raven casually smashed him aside with the thrust of a robotically enhanced arm. He bent down and hauled up Lady Vengeance by the cuffs between her wrists. In the process, he drew her hands away from her bleeding middle, which quickly soaked through the bandages. If it weren't for all the pain, she'd have fallen asleep from the blood loss. She yowled like a dying cat.

"Hurts, does it?" he asked, holding her close. "You ran from your fate last time, but now you'll get what you deserve, murderer."

"Un ... unlikely." Lady Vengeance glanced behind him.

"Oh?" The Raven looked intrigued. "And why do you say that?"

His radar beeped—incoming—and Vivienne seized on the distraction to twist free of his grip. Half a second later, Stardust hit the Raven with a flying tackle that sent the two men careening through the opposite wall. Lady Vengeance fell aside, thrown back by the impact. She landed heavily and felt her ankle twist painfully under her.

"This is so not my day," she murmured.

~

The two armored men tumbled through the wall into the holding cell area, then plowed out the back of the police station and through the opposite wall into Cobalt City's central post office. A bag of mail burst around them, and flying letters turned the world into a snowglobe of paper. All the letters disrupted Stardust's sensors, and he slammed into the ground. The momentary disorientation was enough for the Raven to elbow him in the chest with the force of a crashing semi-truck, and Jaccob flew up, cracked the ceiling, then landed awkwardly on his feet. The Raven struggled up, his shredded black cape clicking like a hundred blades strung together.

"You recovered from the ion blast quickly," the Raven said. "Commendable."

"Jaccobean particles," Stardust said. "And you didn't get broken in half when I tackled you, so your suit must be pretty strong. Props."

The two faced each other, sizing up one another's tech. Stardust had to assume the Raven had been following him for some time—perhaps even since the mall—and that meant his tech was better, at least in terms of stealth. Stardust also had the edge in terms of energy blasts, near as he could figure. But he had the Jaccobean particles, with their unique laws of physics—that was his advantage.

The Raven made the first move, throwing up his cloak like a shield. Stardust raised his arm, thinking he could just send a Starbolt right through, but two scything razors flew from the Raven's cloak and scraped across his blue gauntlet. The first one shot past him into the rubble, and he batted the second down to the ground. It sank at least halfway into the pavement under his feet.

"Careful with those things!" Stardust said. "You might hurt yourself."

He fired a Starbolt at the Raven, but watched, dumbfounded, as it drained away—seemingly absorbed into the man's armor.

"Now that's just not fair—" he started to say, but the Raven ran toward him, leaped, and kicked him in the chest with both enhanced feet. He flew backward and sank into the brick wall next to the huge hole they'd smashed leading into the alley.

The armor absorbed the shock, but he'd definitely felt that one. "Ow."

The Raven stood over him, dust rising like smoke around his forbidding visage. "I have no quarrel with you, Jaccob Stevens," he said. "Do not interfere further."

Stardust blasted him with two more Starbolts to as much effect as before. If anything, it seemed to power *up* the Raven's armor.

"Interfere with *what*, you trying to kill someone?" he asked. "You're the asshole who ripped her open, aren't you? You think I'm going to let you get away with that?"

"I am doing what must be done," the Raven said. "You have no idea what that woman is capable of doing. What she has already done."

Keep him talking, Jaccob. At his wordless instruction, the Computer did a targeting layout that showed he had to get the Raven six inches closer. "Whatever it was, it doesn't justify murder."

The Raven took a step closer. "You don't—"

"Target acquired, Stardust," said the Computer. "Have a nice day."

"All power to thrusters," he said, and his boot-jets exploded with enough force to launch him into the stratosphere. He tackled the Raven as he shot up and out.

The Raven struggled a little in Stardust's arms, but even if he fought his way free, then he would be falling, and his suit looked less like a manned flying vehicle and more like an exoskeleton to enhance kicks and punches. At least the change in pressure hadn't suddenly killed him.

When they hit ten thousand feet, Stardust opened up a channel to the Raven's suit. "I don't think ravens fly this high, but comets do," he said. "And since I don't see any jets on your tech, how about we talk, or I lose my grip a little?"

At first, the Raven offered no reply, and Stardust heard only crackling static on the comm-link. Then: "You are fighting the wrong battle, hero. If you have even the slightest concern for the city you claim to protect, you will let me go about my work."

"Yeah, like that's going to happen," Stardust said.

"So be it." The Raven drew out his miniature EMP.

"Hey! Hey, careful with that—"

Then the Raven blasted him, and Stardust's armor shut off—as did the Raven's. Their upward momentum slowed, stopped, and they started falling.

CHAPTER FIVE

HEARING VOICES

"Are you crazy?" Stardust shouted. "Now we're *both* going to die!"

The Raven couldn't have heard, with the comm-link depowered and the wind whipping past their heads, but he replied by kicking off Stardust, sending them both into crazy spins. The Raven drifted away, then spread his arms and cloak into a glider.

"Oh great," Stardust said as he streaked past the Raven toward Cobalt City. "Computer? Hey. Hey!"

"I'm working on it, Stardust," the Computer said. "Fifteen seconds. Would you like a massage this time to help you relax?"

"No, I don't—dammit, disable that feature!"

"Yes, Stardust. Nine seconds."

His armor had adapted to the EMP, so the recharge wouldn't be as long, but damn, he'd really have to do something about *this* bullshit. If, that is, his armor came back up in time to pull up and not make a twenty-foot Stardust-shaped crater in the ground. He tried to avoid doing the math about whether he would bounce two times or three times. And failed.

The Raven soared down, directing his flight toward the smoking part of the city—where they had just been fighting. If Stardust couldn't get there in time ...

"Six seconds," the Computer said in her cheerful, sexy voice.

"Come on," he said, as the seconds ticked off. There was a bar for the power charge, and he watched it creep slowly toward complete. Too slowly.

"Five seconds."

The ground was getting larger. He could make out individual buildings.

"Four seconds."

He was going to land down by the docks, so at least the casualties would be low.

"Three seconds."

No, scratch that. Winds were pushing him off course, and he was headed for ... oh great, downtown. During rush hour.

"Two seconds."

He could distinguish cars.

"One second."

"Come on!" he shouted, as he could see people now, looking up in terror at the comet rushing toward them. "Come on!"

"Stand by," the Computer said reasonably.

"Stand by?" Stardust screamed. "What do you mean, stand—?"

His boot-jets roared to life.

"Full power," said the Computer. "And you were worried."

Stardust pulled up steeply and managed to divert his course so that instead of crashing into a major intersection, he took out a nearby parking garage. Cars went flying, and people shrieked as they ran for cover. Stardust broke through one, two, three, then four levels of the parking garage, until he finally found himself lying on the ground—battered and dented—next to a parking attendant's booth. The woman regarded him, somewhat unsurprised. Apparently, she'd seen it all, and was waiting for a toll.

"I left my wallet in my other power suit," he said. "Bill me?"

She nodded and pushed the button to raise the exit bar.

Stardust shot out of the parking garage, roared up the street, and directed himself back to the police station. Maybe the Raven hadn't got back yet ... *yes*! His radar showed a human-sized vehicle gliding in from the opposite direction. He wasn't headed for the hole in the station, though, but rather for the roof, where Stardust's armor picked up another human signature, this one female. He understood what that might mean and hoped he was wrong.

Stardust set in new coordinates and flew up to the police station roof. There stood Lady Vengeance, her hand outstretched toward the Raven, who was gliding in like a bird of prey. Didn't she know how dangerous he was? He was going to kill her!

~

As the Raven swooped in, Lady Vengeance knew she would only get one shot at this. She couldn't control her powers a hundred percent, as the power dampener still had some wearing off to do. But there was no choice. She dug deep, drank of as much fear as she could in the surrounding area, and focused on holding it.

Downstairs, police were talking down terrified visitors and inmates. Down in the street, children were crying, and startled commuters were trying desperately to get through the growing traffic jam. Vivienne absorbed it all. The media would show up soon, and then all the fear would turn into fascination, and then she would be sunk.

"Not enough," she whispered. "There's not enough."

There's always me, came another voice—not her own, but one she'd heard far too many times. Usually, alcohol kept that voice at bay, but she hadn't had a drink since Colorado. Maybe after escaping the mall, she should have robbed a liquor store, but bandages had seemed more important at the time. Mistake.

She channeled the fear and looked up at the Raven. This was it. She—

Unfortunately, the sound of Stardust's approaching boot-jets distracted her—God, was he *loud*—and the Raven hit her before she could refocus. They went rolling across the gravelly rooftop. They broke apart and faced each other, each breathing hard.

The Raven looked worse-for-wear. His battered armor had powered down, and ice still clung to the helmet, meaning he must have been up a long way when the de-icing system had failed. Vivienne's insides felt like seared hamburger stuck in the blender, but at least they weren't falling out. The Raven must have shorted out his nanobot suppressor somehow, or maybe she had Sparklemotion to thank for that. Either way, Vivienne had to stop the Raven here, or he'd keep coming and coming. Now that he was injured and his armor partly depowered seemed her best chance.

"Old school, huh?" she said, flexing her claw. "I can do that."

The Raven had a strong mind, but a little fear coiled. Lady Vengeance siphoned that and reshaped it into a swirling black-and-purple sword in her hand.

"A fearsword? Hardly fair." The Raven's craggy voice made her heart race.

"You can always give up."

"Never." His shoulders heaved. His one red eye stared at her unblinking.

Kill him, said the voice. *Kill him, or he will kill you.*

As though her body was listening even if her mind wasn't, she raised the sword toward the Raven. One little cut—that's all it would take. She'd paralyze him, then finish him off while he tried to escape the fear-coma. *Yes*, the voice said. *Kill him.*

Vivienne fought the voice. "Please, just let me go. I don't want to hurt you."

The Raven hesitated. "I—"

Then Stardust's hand fell on her shoulder. "Stand down," he projected. "*Now.*"

The Raven had always been quick to react. As Lady Vengeance paused, the Raven lunged at her, and it was *Stardust* that saved her. The armored hero put himself between the two—whether out of instinct or dumb luck, she couldn't say—and the black talons scraped against Stardust's head, tearing off his helmet. If he hadn't been there, the Raven would have clawed Lady Vengeance's head clean off.

Stardust pointed his blaster at the Raven's face. "Stop it!" he shouted. "You—"

"Wait!" Without thinking, Lady Vengeance grabbed Stardust's raised arm, turned it downward, and redirected his Starbolt into the rooftop around their feet. Stardust's blast cut the roof apart, and the Raven flailed down into the collapsing rubble. The Raven's red eye locked on her until he vanished amongst the dust, brick, and wood. She stared back, hardly remembering to breathe, as Stardust grabbed her in both arms and hovered above the crater in the roof.

"Damn," Stardust said. "What did you just do?"

"I didn't kill him." Lady Vengeance blinked. "His armor will protect him. It has to."

"What?" Stardust looked as confused as he sounded.

He looked acutely uncomfortable floating there with a woman in his arms who was not his wife. Also, this was the first time she'd properly seen his face, and she had to confess he was pretty good-looking in the fading afternoon light, in a geeky way.

Shame. Why did all the good ones have to be taken?

Lady Vengeance smiled at him. "Sorry, Shiny."

"For what, not killing him? That's quite all right. In fact, I encourage *not* killing."

"Not for that." She shook her head. "This."

Lady Vengeance reached up and kissed him on the lips. As she did, her eyes lit with black fire, and she plunged the remains of her fearsword into his side.

~

As she kissed him, Stardust felt pressure inside his head, like an approaching migraine headache. Lady Vengeance seemed to have disappeared. He looked around, blearily, trying to figure out what was going on. Did the big apartment building shudder just then? Sure enough, it sprouted limbs of brick, plumbing, and electrical wires.

"No way," Stardust said.

Then the apartment building picked up the post office and hit him with it.

He flew backward off the roof and crash-landed in the middle of the street. Cars swerved aside as he rolled to a stop, and drivers abandoned their vehicles to run screaming from the huge traffic jam.

"What?" Stardust asked as he started to rise.

Then something knocked him back to the ground. He barely managed to roll aside before a massive force stomped down where he had been. A nearby Ford had reared up over him like a bear on its hind legs, and now it looked like it wanted Stardust pâté. Other cars were making their way toward him, equally intent on squashing the hero. Fire hydrants blew their tops and sprayed water at him, while traffic lights came unhinged to swing down like pendulums. All along the street, buildings pulled free of their foundations, the better to press the attack.

Technical genius that he was, Jaccob Stevens had made his Stardust armor tough enough to withstand the rigors of space travel and re-entry. He was physically prepared for the impact of bullets, speeding cars, and even the occasional meteor. He was not, however, *mentally* prepared for the shock of one building clobbering him with another, much less all the cars, buildings, and utility installations rising up and join the assault. It was as though his beloved Cobalt City—the place he had sworn to defend to his dying breath—had tired of his stewardship and decided to kill him. Deep, soul-wrenching horror filled him, so intense that it stunned him to catatonic stillness.

"Computer," he said as he dodged a semi. "What's going on? What—?"

"I'm not sure I understand the question, Stardust," she said. "Please rephrase?"

"What's making everything come to life and attack me?"

"I am not sure I know what you mean, Stardust," the Computer said. "You're lying in the street having muscle spasms. People are staring, and a news crew is on its way."

"News crew? What—?"

"From a PR standpoint, you might want to get up and rejoin the fight."

Then he understood. He was caught in another of Lady Vengeance's illusions, this one much more powerful than Chuck's kidnapping. None of this was really happening—it was all in his mind. He closed his eyes, dug in deep, and stopped trying to dodge the attacking city. And sure enough, no blows came. When he opened his eyes, the vision was gone, and he was standing in the middle of the street, surrounded by hundreds of onlookers with flashing cameras. His little illusory fit would probably be on the 6 o'clock news, if the videos hadn't gone viral on the Internet already.

"I *hate* magic," he said.

His boot-jets fired, and he flew up to the roof. No sign of either of them.

"Great."

~

Deep in the heart of a collapsed building, the Raven shook himself awake inside his rubble prison. This Stardust was proving quite a problem—one that would need more recon before a solution could be found.

Afternoon had given way to evening, and he heard the voices of rescue crews surveying the damage and looking for survivors. The Raven's movements were restricted, but he could still reach the little buttons on the inside of his wrists, which he pressed simultaneously. With a hiss, his armor shifted then retracted, snake-like, into a small power pack nestled at the small of his back. The added wiggle room helped as he squirmed free of the rubble.

"Here," he called. "I'm here!"

Two men in orange coats that said CCFD hurried into the room and helped the middle-aged Hispanic man out of the rubble. He looked confused, with his eyes pointing subtly in two different directions. Though he *seemed* helpless, he pulled himself out of the rubble as though he hardly needed help from the firemen. Once they had him free, another cry for help sounded elsewhere in the building.

"I'll be fine," he said. "Just go."

The firemen started away, but one turned back. "We have to get you down to the paramedics ... sir?"

The Raven was long gone.

CHAPTER SIX

SPIRIT OF STARCOM

"Wow." Vivienne stared up at Starcom Tower as the sun set that evening, casting the long shadow of the building across the park. "Compensating, much?"

It wasn't the biggest structure she'd ever seen. The sheer Cyclopean scale of elder gods warranted bigger temples, and ancient alien civilizations tended to move in ships the size of Rhode Island. Even on earth, people built bigger buildings: the skyscrapers of New York, the excesses of Dubai, the pyramids. But *damn.* Starcom Tower had a certain *presence* to it. It exuded power to let everyone within fifty miles know that Jaccob Stevens was the biggest dude around.

"Definitely compensating," she said, and took a swig of bourbon.

Jaccob Stevens, that was the name. Ten minutes at an Internet café had yielded plenty of information about him, Starcom Industries, and Cobalt City's recent past. The team of heroes called the Protectorate had gone silent after certain tragic events a few years ago, but its wealthiest and most popular member, Jaccob Stevens—a.k.a. Stardust—kept kicking villainous butt and taking names. In his day job, Jaccob ran a multi-billion-dollar technology empire that ran the gamut in products from cellular and satellite communications to military-level supply. Obviously the Stardust armor was the Holy Grail of Starcom's offerings, but Jaccob kept that under tight security. It wasn't like boys to share their toys, after all.

Interestingly, Jaccob was not actually the CEO of his own company: his wife, Elizabeth Stevens, had run Starcom while he played hero, though there was a gradual transition happening now. Informally, Elizabeth meant to announce her "retirement" within the year to focus on a philanthropy project called "World Armor," naming Jaccob as her replacement as CEO of Starcom. For his part, Jaccob seemed to be resisting the changeover stubbornly. He didn't seem ready to let go of being a hero. Vivienne filed that information away for future use.

This whole day had sucked hard. She hadn't seen the Raven since the fight at the police station earlier, but she knew he was still out there. Enough time had passed for the nanobots to fix her up and her powers to come back—thank God—but he so clearly overpowered her that she didn't want to fight him, nor did she want something to go wrong and hurt him. The whole situation was so hopelessly *fucked* that coming to Starcom actually made sense. And that was just crazy.

But at least Stardust wouldn't shove her head-first into a wood chipper the second he saw her—he didn't know her that well—so this seemed like the best bet.

"Vivienne, you are insane," she murmured as she crossed the expansive lobby. "Totally, fucking, pound-my-head-against-a-wall—"

"Can I help you?" said a cheerful, handsome man at the front desk.

Vivienne sized him up quickly: late twenties/early thirties, immaculately dressed and groomed, Bluetooth buckled to his ear. Her empath powers picked up on his emotions as well, which had a lot to do with his boyfriend back at home. No flirting with this one, alas. The best she could hope for was trying not to seem like a crazy homeless person in a black leather jacket.

"Hi," she said, slurring the word as little as possible. "I'd like to see Mr. Stevens. It's personal business. Unexpected. Urgent. Any availability?"

"Right you are, ma'am." He clicked on his computer.

Ma'am? Seriously? Vivienne made a mental note to do a better job with her makeup—when she wasn't on the run for her life, of course.

"Hmm." The receptionist looked sad. "I checked his schedule, but Mr. Stevens appears to have cancelled all his appointments to schedule 'patrol time!' with an exclamation point. You know what that means." He offered Vivienne a dreamy smile. "He's out jetting around in those metal hot pants of his. Rowr."

"Oh, don't I know it." Damn. Stardust not being in the building was a good thing if she intended to break in, but not so much if she had to talk to him.

"Can I schedule you later in the week? It looks like Tuesday after 3 p.m. but before 4:30 p.m. is open. Or maybe you'd prefer a morning appointment, such as Wednesday at 10:12? 11:00? 11:12? Mr. Stevens likes to meet in twelve-minute increments. I'll call his assistant Marjorie—"

"No, that's fine," she said, her head starting to ache from the details. God, this kid talked really fast, and she was entirely too tipsy for this. "I'll just go."

"I thought you said it was urgent."

Damn again. "Not that urgent, just—" Already she could feel the security guards looking speculatively in her direction. "I need to pee. Bathroom?"

Looking a little confused, the receptionist pointed her to a space-age restroom near the elevators, into which she ducked. The bathroom was like something out of *Flash Gordon* by way of *Lifestyles of the Rich and Famous*. Fluffy, warmed towels waited next to the mortar-and-pestle shaped basins, and LCD read-outs measured how clean one's hands were. Vivienne stared at herself in one of the satellite TV mirrors.

"Real subtle, V," she said. "Practically *tell* the kid you're a super-villain sneaking in to ambush his boss. That'll go great." She shook her head. "What you need now is—"

A sexy female voice interrupted her. "What can I do for you, Ms. Cain?"

Vivienne froze. She didn't see anyone in the mirror, but when she looked around, there was a small robot hovering at about knee-level. It was vaguely feminine in shape, sort of like a Cabbage Patch doll.

"Would you like fresh towels, Ms. Cain?" asked the robot. "A massage, perhaps?"

"No," she said. "How—how do you know my name?"

"You are flagged in Starcom's archives," the robot said. "Tea or coffee?" Part of the robot unfolded into a miniature espresso machine.

"Um, no thanks." Vivienne felt unnerved about being so readily identified. "Are you the Computer he was talking to earlier? In the armor?"

"I am a single system with many operating interfaces and multiple memory backups," the Computer said. "The Stardust armor memory is uploaded at regular intervals." The robot trailed off, as though that answered the full question

"Has it been ... uploaded from today?" Her powers didn't work well against machines—no fear to be absorbed—but she palmed her silver claw.

"No, updates occur at midnight," the Computer said. "And if you intend to use that weapon against this device, I recommend against it. The bathroom attendant device may not seem combat-equipped, but my disruptor is more than capable of disintegrating a human of your height and weight. Or more likely, stunning you until the authorities arrive." The robot—with that voice, it was hard not to think of it as "she"—started pouring a cup of hot water. "Are you sure you won't take tea?"

"Sure, why not?" Vivienne said. "Um—"

"Your heart rate is elevated, and you are breathing heavily. Rest assured, you are not flagged as a threat or denied access. I will take no action to hinder you."

"Uh huh." Vivienne suspected the Computer would say exactly something like that to cover a silent alarm.

The Computer continued. "Besides—Stark says you're all right."

"Stark? Like, short for Starcom? Isn't that you?"

"I am the Computer," she said. "Stark is Stark."

Before Vivienne could further this line of questioning, heels clicked on the linoleum outside the door, warning of an imminent arrival. "Gotta go."

"But your tea," said the Computer.

"Fuck the tea."

Vivienne took refuge in one of the bathroom stalls, which contained honest-to-God ceramic toilets. They weren't the industrial toilets she might expect, but something one might find in a comfortable chateau: extended seats and even arm rests. She pulled the lid off the back of the toilet to expose plenty of room around the inner workings and she almost stashed her claw in there. She might need it, though.

Through the crack between the door and the next stall, she watched the robot whirring thoughtfully, confused by her instruction, and then the far door opened.

The receptionist's voice drifted in. "I'll make sure to have him call when he gets in, ma'am—"

"No worries, David," a blonde woman in the doorway called back. "If he's got his comm-link turned off, it means he's in the zone. I'll catch him eventually." She shut the door and shook her head. "Ma'am? Seriously?"

"Welcome, Liz," the Computer said to her. "Tea?"

"Please," said the blonde woman—Liz. "You already have some ready. Has Jaccob been working on those precognition protocols again?"

"He has not, Liz."

"Hmm."

The blonde took the tea and adjusted her Farrah Fawcett hair in the mirror. This Liz was tall, 40ish, and naturally *Cosmo*-level gorgeous. Liz probably could have modeled in less tasteful magazines about twenty years ago. Vivienne—who well remembered a certain poorly thought-out, infamous Ms. October centerfold shoot from her youth—gave her respect for staving off age. The liquor was dulling Vivienne's empathic absorption a little, but the vibe she got off Liz was cool, if a little irked.

Slowly, Vivienne put the lid of the toilet back into place, taking care not to make any sound as she did so. It just wouldn't do to listen in while holding that huge thing.

"I don't know what that man's got in his head," Liz said. "Out jetting around to all hours, never answering his phone, not telling me what's going on. He tells me to take the kids and go to the cabin, even though it's clearly on the calendar that I have meetings this afternoon. It's like he's on a mission to be annoying. What do you think, Computer?"

The Computer beeped. "Jaccob's recent behavior falls entirely within the parameters of his psychological profile."

"Yes, that's what I'm afraid of."

This "Liz" sounded vaguely familiar, as if Vivienne had heard her voice before. She sat down on the toilet and drew her feet up to hide behind the door and think. Maybe if she waited around, the woman would just go away. Not that time was on her side, with sobriety creeping back in. Coming down off her last dose of anti-depressants—over twenty-four hours ago—wasn't helping any. Maybe this "Liz" had valium or something. These trophy wife types always did.

Vivienne reached into her coat and pulled out the little bottle of bourbon she'd managed to pick up at a liquor store when its owner ran away screaming "Snakes! Why did it have to be *snakes*!" Fear powers were so useful, if unpredictable. She took a long pull on the bottle and tried to relax.

It was then that Vivienne felt something in the bathroom stall with her. Not a presence, exactly—she'd faced ghosts before, as well as people who could turn invisible or intangible just by thinking about it—but definitely a *something*. She could feel its emotions all around her: warm and uneasy. Determining if she was a threat.

"Stark," she murmured. "I get it."

At her voice, the spirit of Starcom Tower drew away. Vivienne imagined most people never came close to interacting with it. Contacting an animist spirit took a certain level of psychic chops at the best of times, and there were so many businesses in Starcom Tower that the poor thing probably suffered from serious dissociative identity disorder anyway. Vivienne sent out some sympathy and received a warm feeling in return. Or maybe that was lithium withdrawal. Hurk.

The urge to hurl the contents of her stomach—mostly liquor, to be fair—rose in Vivienne, and she gagged to keep from doing it.

"Hello?" said Liz. "Is someone there?"

"Crap."

Vivienne couldn't help smiling at the sheer idiocy of it all. Here she was, half-drunk, hiding in the bathroom of a superhero who'd blasted and arrested her earlier that day, and she'd just had the sort of awkward experience of being caught eavesdropping on some woman who'd thought herself alone. Maybe she could murmur something unintelligible, and then they'd part ways and feel weird about it all day. Or she could pretend not to be there, but that would probably be even weirder.

"Hi," Vivienne said. "I'm sorry, I didn't—I didn't want to interrupt."

"Oh, that's fine." Liz didn't sound at all bothered. "It's just my husband. Men, right?"

"Pretty much." Vivienne had a thought in the depths of the growing influence of the bourbon: a bunch of things connecting themselves. Google at the internet café, her voice, what the receptionist had said, the words "Jaccob" and "husband." "Hey. Don't take this the wrong way, but are you Elizabeth Stevens? Like, Mrs. Stardust?"

"Heh," Liz said. "I guess I am. Why?"

"Oh, no reason." Again, Vivienne slid the ceramic cover off the back of the toilet. Then she shoved the door open and strode into the bathroom, shaping her stored fear energy. "Sorry about this. You seem nice."

Liz backed a step away, surprised, not afraid. "You're her, aren't you? The goth-dressing, dimension-hopping super-villain Jaccob fought earlier." Her nose crinkled at the whisky bottle in her jacket pocket. "You smell like a liquor cabinet."

"Hey, I don't—oh, fuck it." She touched Liz's arm, and the blonde woman sank to the ground, trapped in a nightmare. Vivienne caught her and eased her down, which was difficult with the lid of a toilet hanging from one hand. She managed it awkwardly.

"Wow," Vivienne said. "And here I thought Stardust was just a geek with toys. How'd he land such a hottie?" She paused. "I feel like I'm forgetting something—"

The bathroom attendant robot whirred angrily at the woman who had just attacked its master. It was unfolding a disruptor projector, as promised. "Alert! Alert!"

"Oh yeah." Vivienne brought down the ceramic toilet lid down on the robot's head. The robot crunched, warbled a couple more muted alerts, then died.

Vivienne sat down heavily on the linoleum floor. “I am so bad at this whole kidnapping people thing,” she said.

She took another swig of bourbon. “OK, what now?”

PART TWO

HERO ANGST

CHAPTER SEVEN

INDUSTRIAL ESPIONAGE

Three days later, Jaccob leaned back in his office chair, looked around at all the framed newspaper articles on the walls, and sighed. "This sucks."

Nothing at Starcom prompted his malaise. It was a normal day at the office, in his sumptuous executive suite just downstairs from the penthouse. He'd had a good instinct, telling Liz to take the kids to the cabin for a few days, but it meant he couldn't work from home. It would start off fine, but he would inevitably get restless and waste all his time on video games without someone to tell him to focus. Here, the task fell to his secretary: a pretty, strawberry-blonde friend-of-the-family named Marjorie, who used to babysit Chuck and Mike when they were young. He'd instructed her to interrupt him periodically so his mind wouldn't wander. At least there were no video games to distract him at his office—he'd had Liz design the firewall so that he couldn't break it and download some onto his work computer. His wife had always been smarter than he was, which explained a lot about Starcom, really.

He checked his messages, but there was nothing from his wife. She knew how he got when there was "something big" going on, and she wouldn't bother him until he got it out of his system. He'd meant to call her several times in the last couple days, but always forgot about it until two in the morning. He'd fly out to the cabin after work and check on Liz and the kids.

The schematics on his computer were actually extremely interesting. Starcom was in the final development stages of a new radar system for the U.S. Government—one that detected drones as tiny as a basketball. Jaccob himself had excitedly designed most of it (with substantial help from Liz, of course), but since this whole Lady Vengeance vs. the Raven thing had come up, he'd barely even thought about the lab. He hoped the engineers knew what they were doing.

No, the reason for Jaccob's boredom was that he wanted to be out there, hunting down one or the other of the dangerous supers messing up Cobalt City. Not that he could, with all the work he had to do in the office, all the repairs and upgrades he had to make on his armor, and his raging inability to find either the Raven or Lady Vengeance.

In the last three days, sightings of the Raven plastered the news. A black-armored vigilante was out taking down criminals, shaking down the Underworld to find a certain dark-haired femme fatale. The police had no hope of stopping the Raven, and he'd left more than a few officers ruthlessly incapacitated if not permanently damaged. No one could stand in his way—at least for long.

As for Lady Vengeance, she'd disappeared entirely.

Jaccob had gone out in backup Stardust armor every night, staying up until the extremely wee hours, but both the Raven and Lady Vengeance seemed more than capable of dodging his surveillance. None of his contacts—mostly new superheroes who'd taken up the mantle after the Protectorate dissolved—had been able to turn up anything, and honestly, he was glad. He didn't feel comfortable sending kids against someone like the Raven, so after discreet inquiries, he'd advised any would-be vigilantes to back off and let him handle it. Fortunately, they'd agreed. What he really needed was the Protectorate, with its diverse skillset. Subtlety and recon (other than laser-marking targets for his Starbolts) were not on Stardust's list of specialties.

He wanted to spend every moment looking for these disruptions to his city. He wouldn't have even been at the office if it hadn't been for his responsibilities.

Jaccob couldn't focus on what he was supposed to be doing. "Computer," he said. "Call up previous search results on the Raven."

"Right away, Jaccob."

The data on his screen was scant, but it told Jaccob where he'd heard the name before. The Raven (technically the Raven III, as there'd been two previous wearers of the mantle) was a crazy ex-superhero—non-public, secretive, armored-vigilante type. He'd formerly belonged to a team called Supergroup, but they broke up almost twenty years ago, and he moved to Colorado to enforce his brand of justice across the western half of the United States.

Worse, he got into politics. Around five years ago, the Raven made headlines when he won a write-in election for Colorado's governor, drawing support from right-wing militias and left-wing techies alike. With the outpouring of public support (which he didn't even ask for), he took over Colorado and turned much of it into his own private martial-law city-state called Valhalla. The U.S. bowed to the state of things: so long as Colorado stayed a nominal part of the union, followed federal law, and paid taxes, the Raven was granted relative autonomy.

The huge cultural event sent ripples through the superhero community, but it was even bigger in the tech industry. At first, the U.S. considered military intervention to depose the rogue state, but their planes and killer drones shut off at the border: just fell out of the sky. It turned out the Raven had installed ionizing technology (the same thing that had knocked Stardust on his butt) in the Rockies and used it against all incoming tech except his own. The sheer technological accomplishment was staggering. In terms of innovation on the bleeding edge, Valhalla might have proved a strong rival to Starcom, if it had any interest in affairs outside its own borders.

Before three days ago, Jaccob had never had the pleasure of meeting the Raven in person. Now that he had, he understood why Valhalla had earned a reputation for being as impenetrable and unpredictable as North Korea. He could find no official information about the Raven's out-of-costume identity, if he even *had* one.

He sat back in his chair. "Now Lady Vengeance," he said. "Vivienne Cain."

The Computer had a little more about Lady Vengeance: punk/goth heroine, also a former member of Supergroup, fear powers, tabloid darling of the 90s. She'd apparently dated some pretty big names in the movie and music biz, but there was no record of any long-term relationships. Details of her crazy media stunts filled volumes, from wardrobe malfunctions ("Heroine Loses Battle, Shirt") to scandalous photo shoots ("Scary Sexy: Lady

Vengeance *is* Ms. October") to her short-lived musical career ("Superhero Songstress Clashes with Wildebeast Villain on Stage, Vomits on Crowd"). Some of the articles made him chuckle, and some made him blush.

None of them told him how to find her, though. That first day, people all over town had reported strange hallucinations and nightmares, but after that, it had faded. Perhaps Lady Vengeance had left the city, or—as seemed more likely—she'd regained control of her powers and was lying low. She had to be in Cobalt City somewhere—the Raven would have gone if she had left or—worse—he'd found and killed her.

At first, Stardust had hoped to trace her with a dedicated tracker—thanks to the kiss, he had some of her DNA—but that had so far proved fruitless. It seemed Lady Vengeance was used to hiding from tech-based heroes, which made sense if she'd spent all those years ducking the Raven.

The dates didn't add up, though. The group had dissolved twenty years before, but the Raven had set up Valhalla a little more than five years ago. What had he been doing in the interim? Chasing Lady Vengeance? If he had a grudge, it was a big one.

"Supergroup," Jaccob said, clicking through links. A superhero team active up until twenty years ago, Supergroup had broken up for the same reason that all superhero teams eventually dissolved: everyone got on everyone else's nerves. The members went their separate ways for a while but held regular reunions every year on the anniversary of the group's dissolution. That is, until one year ...

Jaccob stared at the screen. It suddenly felt colder in his office. Slowly, he clicked through to read an article titled "Supergroup Massacre."

Apparently, the group's tenth and final reunion had ended in tragedy. A small army of the team's rogue's gallery had attacked them all at once, then disappeared seemingly without a trace. Most of the former Supergroup had died in the assault, including Justice, Athena, Aphid, and the previous Raven. The article said only two had survived: the Raven (again, no data on his real name) and ...

Jaccob paged down, expecting to find Lady Vengeance listed, but instead, it was a name he knew only by reputation: Big Head, who was now a chief science advisor at the Pentagon. Another tech hero, though more of a researcher and inventor than a warrior.

Where was Lady Vengeance listed as a survivor? Had she even been there?

The article listed her as missing, presumed dead. What did that mean?

Jaccob shivered.

The intercom startled him with a triumphant little pop-rock ditty—the official Stardust theme music, once all the legalities were worked out. He clicked answer. "Thanks for the wake-up call Marjorie," he said. "Call me back in the next ten minutes?"

"Actually, Sir," the intercom said in Marjorie's voice. "Your 2 o'clock is here."

"First, call me Jaccob, and second, my *what*?"

"Your 2 o'clock appointment, Sir. I'm sorry I didn't remind you, but it looks like you set up the appointment yourself and didn't tell me." There was a hint of reproach in his secretary's voice.

"Oh." He did that often—organization was not one of his skills either—but he had no recollection of setting an appointment for this afternoon. "Who am I meeting?"

"Antonio Desantes, Sir. From IberTech."

The name didn't seem familiar, but Starcom had indeed been getting into some business deals with IberTech. The overseas company was a small but sharp outfit established in Spain and Italy. "Send him in then," he said. "Two minutes."

"Yes, Sir."

"And you can call me Jaccob, Marjorie."

"I know, Sir."

He clicked off the intercom and straightened his tie. With Liz out at the cabin, he'd had to tie it himself this morning, so naturally it looked like a rat's nest. He was a scientific genius, and yet the simple things eluded him. At least Liz had managed to talk him out of Velcro shoes halfway through college—that would have been a disaster at the annual Starcom shareholders meetings.

The thought of Liz made Jaccob smile. At least she and the kids were safe from this whole Raven vs. Lady Vengeance thing. The cabin was a fortress, and any attempt to get in without Stevens DNA to provide the passcode would fail utterly, or at least set off half a dozen alarms here at Starcom Tower.

The intercom buzzed to warn him his two minutes were up, and the door opened to admit a clean-cut, dark-haired man in his early fortics. He was Latino of some extraction. Mexican? Spain-Spanish? He wore a tailored black suit and carried a briefcase, as well as a touch-screen tablet in a holster at his belt. He wore thick glasses and when he spoke, it was with an accent that lisped "S" sounds.

He held out his hand. "Mr. Stevens, it is an honor."

"Oh, Starcom isn't all that." Jaccob smiled as they shook hands. "Granted, we *do* have the biggest tower by volume of the Fortune-500 companies, but who am I to brag?"

Desantes appeared to take the joke as a serious question. "You are the hero Stardust. You are a legend in our industry."

"Aw shucks," he said. "I put my super-powered armor on the same as anyone—one blaster at a time. Then I go fight crime. It's not like I have a Nobel Peace Prize. Though I wouldn't say no, of course."

No one had ever accused Jaccob Stevens of having a *small* ego.

There was something strange about Antonio Desantes, but Jaccob couldn't quite put his finger on it. Something about his face—or his voice? "Your accent—Castilian?"

"*Sí, maestro.*" Desantes nodded. "As we discussed previously, I am here to inspect the Starcom facility, to determine how my company can best work with yours."

"As we discussed?"

Desantes looked at him blankly, and Jaccob realized he'd probably forgotten. He did that fairly often, and over the last few days he'd been more than distracted. Which meant he probably hadn't arranged for anything, either.

"Sure. Hey, I'll take you on a personal tour." He waved away Desantes's immediate, polite objections. "Nah, it'll be good for me. Get my legs moving, you know."

Marjorie took care of the paperwork—Desantes passed export control with flying colors—and Jaccob led them down past the conference rooms to the labs. He didn't show him any of the juicy stuff, of course—Desantes didn't work for him, after all—but there was enough impressive stuff in Starcom Tower for any technician to fall in love. Jaccob had designed it that way: Starcom was his own private geeky wonderland, and he couldn't resist the urge to show things off.

As they walked, Jaccob studied Desantes. The man was obviously very intelligent, and he had a piercing focus that took in every detail. He seemed extremely interested in everything he saw, though he took no notes.

"Even I don't remember everything I'm doing down here," Jaccob said when they stopped for coffee. Desantes had tea. "You must have a photographic memory."

"No, not that." Desantes dipped his bag of Earl Grey in his mug. "Shall we be honest, Mr. Stevens?"

"Please. And call me Jaccob. If I can call you Antonio?"

Desantes nodded. "My company is interested in all these things, but our primary interest is in the Stardust armor."

Jaccob crossed his arms. "And I'm just going to let you in and see that?"

"That depends," he says.

"On?"

"The eternal question," Desantes said. "If you were a hero, would you be able to fly or walk invisibly? Would you be the bold hero, swooping in to save the day, or would you choose to hide from the world, so that none could find you?"

"That's all very poetic and true and all, but what's it mean?"

Desantes set down his tea and took the previously unused tablet out of the holster on his belt. He flicked it on and handed it to Jaccob. Schematics popped up: holographic projectors, light bending apparatus, sound-dampening fields ...

"This ... Wait, is this *stealth* tech? Where did you get this?"

"We have our sources," Desantes said. "Read."

Jaccob scrolled through several pages and came to a drawing of a human with stealth projectors superimposed. His stomach roiled. "Stealth for my armor. OMG."

Desantes opened his briefcase, which was filled with a cybernetic harness that matched the specs on the tablet. "We are prepared to offer you this prototype, in exchange for the opportunity to study—"

"Done." Jaccob took the briefcase. "I'll supervise you personally, of course."

"Of course," Desantes agreed. "For now, perhaps—what do you Americans say? A peek?"

"We can do that, sure."

Jaccob led him to the observation room in the lab, his mind whirling with the possibilities. He didn't watch Desantes all that closely, but there was a wall of unbreakable glass between him and the workshop.

After a few minutes, Desantes nodded in satisfaction. "I shall return tomorrow?"

Jaccob nodded, then they shook hands and parted ways.

"Flying *and* invisibility," Jaccob said. "*Outstanding.*"

This would really help with the subtlety issue.

It wasn't until after he left that evening that Jaccob realized what it was about Desantes that had seemed odd. His eyes didn't quite match. The shades were very close—both of them dark brown in color—but they didn't focus on the same thing at the same time. Perhaps one of the eyes was glass.

He quickly forgot all about it.

~

Antonio Desantes spent the next two hours familiarizing himself with Starcom: the layout, the products, and the like. He couldn't directly study the Stardust armor without Jaccob's personal escort, of course, but his clearance allowed him into the labs. He established a reputation that afternoon as a quiet, intriguing foreigner who kept to himself and occasionally tapped a command or two on his tablet computer.

Of course, if they'd known he was hacking into Starcom's systems, it might have been otherwise.

Antonio waited to activate the bug he'd planted in the private lab until Stevens left the building, of course, in case the man had a means of detecting it. Once his personal radar showed Jaccob out of the building for the evening, obviously distracted with the possibilities of the new tech, Antonio could hack in at his leisure. Any analyses, diagnostics, and simple base engineering would get transmitted directly to the HUD he wore under his tailored suit jacket. He could analyze the basic specs of the power suit, which was still there for repairs. It had been stripped of all the fripperies, which would have raised red flags anyway, but the core was there. He looked at the dented piece of metal and imagined its essential system with all its mechanics, programming, and—most importantly—its backdoors. They were all waiting for him, unwatched and vulnerable.

Just when he'd got a taste, however, he slammed into Stardust's firewall.

"Access denied," said a cheery feminine voice. "Good day!"

So Stevens had a computer system in place that matched his tech. Good boy.

Antonio sent attack spikes to erode the Computer's defenses a little. She was tough, this Computer. He launched one of his own personal viruses: *razorwing.exe*, which had never failed him. It disrupted the program's logic functions, rerouting its decision-making processes. In this case, it made the Computer exclaim random things through his tablet.

"I just wanted to hold you in my arms!" she protested in a sing-song voice. "Now is the winter of our mild discomfort! The birds is coming! I like cheese, by the way!"

Antonio turned the volume down and inputted a few more commands.

The Computer wavered, about to yield, but all of a sudden, a pressure built in Antonio's head and the world blurred around him for a second. When it cleared, the program had failed. That almost felt like magic, but what could have done that?

Regardless, the spike hadn't worked, and he would need a direct interface now. Time for plan B. He made his way back to the elevator.

"Going up, please," he said to the voice-activated software.

On the top floor, Stevens' secretary Marjorie looked surprised and somewhat pleased to see him. "Oh, Mr. Desantes! Are you having trouble with your badge?"

"It's perfect." Antonio smiled at her and put his hand on the desk next to hers. "Marjorie, was it?"

She nodded.

"*Bellísima*," he said. "Is Mr. Stevens in? I had one last question for him."

Her face fell. "I'm sorry, he's left for the day."

"I see." Antonio nodded. "May I use your restroom?"

Marjorie nodded and pointed toward the restroom adjoining the waiting room. Antonio went inside, locked the door behind him, and slipped out his wallet. He selected a credit card, with what looked like two waxy adhesive strips like the sort that attach the card to the welcome letter. He slowly peeled them off.

When Antonio left the bathroom, he didn't say a word. He just crossed to Marjorie's desk and sat down on it. She blushed and looked determinedly at her computer. "I, uh—excuse me, Mr. Desantes—"

He stopped her lips with one finger, then knelt beside her. She stared at him, big blue eyes wide. He fixed her with his intense gaze, drew her hand to his lips, and kissed it. Marjorie blinked at him, confused. Antonio said nothing, but merely smiled at her.

"Mr. Desantes." She giggled, then her eyes narrowed slightly. "Sorry, I—"

Marjorie rose to head for the bathroom. No doubt she thought that was what she needed. He counted to three, then got up and followed her. She made it ten feet, staggered woozily, and then fainted. Antonio caught her smoothly and carried her the rest of the way into the bathroom. He made sure she was comfortable.

He paused at the mirror. There was no more purpose in disguising himself, so he let his smile slip away, then silently peeled the contact poison strips from his lips. If he'd talked, he would have poisoned himself. Fortunately, he'd had no real cause to speak—the Raven, after all, only spoke when strictly necessary.

With Marjorie's enhanced security badge, the Raven walked right into Jaccob Stevens' office, took a seat in Jaccob Stevens' chair, and powered on Jaccob Stevens' computer. He tapped in a few commands and fed it some of the information from his HUD. The encryption unraveled.

"Computer," he said.

"Yes, Raven," said a sexy feminine voice from the machine.

"*The* Raven."

"Yes, the Raven. Command?"

"Deactivate firewall," he said. "Bring up all the Starcom specs."

"That's a large amount of data," the Computer said. "Are you sure?"

"Will it cause you to run slowly?" he asked.

"No, the Raven." He could have sworn the Computer made a little snotty laugh.

"Execute," he said. "Redirect specs to the information account I designate."

He tapped in an address on the computer, and just like that, all of Starcom's data started flooding Valhalla's network. It was a lot of data and would take some time, but Marjorie would be out for hours yet.

"M. Process this data," he said into his comm-link. "Find backdoors."

"*Sí, Capitán,*" came the prompt reply.

The Raven leaned back in the chair and looked around Stardust's office. The man kept numerous news articles about himself as Stardust framed on the walls, which the Raven at first took for a collection of trophies. His predecessor—a man he had loved and respected like a father—had kept such a collection as well, and the Raven preserved it as a matter of honor. But on closer inspection, he realized the articles were not complimentary: "Armored hero blows up police station," and "Stardust repulsors cause tenement fire; no injuries reported," and "COO bungles ground breaking ceremony, causes earthquake."

What kind of a man records his failures?

"A good man," the Raven murmured.

The computer beeped, and his eye shot to the screen. Lady Vengeance popped up there, and a description of Stardust's most recent encounter with her. Apparently, she had disappeared, and he had systematically searched the entire city for her. The Raven had failed to find her as well. There was, however, a voicemail message on his work phone from Liz Stevens regarding Lady Vengeance, sent only half an hour ago. Stardust would not have got this message, because the Raven had cut the Computer off from his armor before then. He clicked and listened to the message. And nodded.

The Raven activated his comm-link. "H. Prep a Harrier. Get here as soon as possible. You and M both."

He looked out the window over Cobalt City.

"Soon, Vivienne Cain," he said. "Soon."

CHAPTER EIGHT

THE IMPORTANCE OF FAMILY

With the light backup suit set on autopilot and his mind so busy reviewing the schematics for IberTech's stealth suit (light-bending broadcasters—fantastic!), Jaccob didn't realize he was almost at the cabin until the defenses kicked on and the Computer warned him he was being scanned and missiles were being directed his way. He wondered if he turned on the stealth tech—which he'd installed as a matter of course—whether the defenses would even have registered him?

Fortunately for him, the program was set for his DNA, and he didn't need to do anything to get access. Jaccob appreciated the proximity warning, because it reminded him how pissed Liz could get when he pulled one of his manual landings and took out a tree, the deck furniture, or possibly the pool. "Computer, calculate landing vector."

Her reply came sluggishly. "Calculating, Jaccob."

"Is anything wrong?" Jaccob asked. "You haven't been yourself since the office. Run a diagnostic."

"I am functioning normally, Jaccob," the Computer said. "Honestly."

He nodded, though her standoffish behavior still struck him as odd. No more odd, he supposed, than using the word "honestly." Privately, he suspected the Computer was considerably more intelligent than he had designed her. If she was sluggish, it was probably because she was spending time with her imaginary friend, "Stark." He took a mental note to see about getting rid of that bug.

The cabin was a small, stylish affair out by the lake about fifty miles from Cobalt City. The nearest neighbors were several miles away, and the defensive net cordoned off a wide area where they could relax in perfect security. The architecture of the cabin was decidedly modern, with mostly glass walls to allow a sweeping view of the beautiful area. Of course, Jaccob had built a substantial game room and swimming pool for the kids, a tennis court for Liz (to which he occasionally vocally credited her buns of steel and she returned a long-suffering look), and an eight-person personal theater in the basement for himself. It was where the Stevens family came to get away, though it was of course substantially wired and fully operational for telecommuting, and school was an hour by car or ten minutes by power suit.

He couldn't shake a faint annoyance that he had to go check on Liz and the kids. He wanted to be out there hunting the Raven and Lady Vengeance—being Stardust and protecting Cobalt City. The family was really proving a hindrance.

Also, he couldn't stop thinking about Lady Vengeance kissing him. The earnest way she'd pressed her body against him, both strong and damaged at the same time ... Aside from magical compulsions and such, Jaccob Stevens couldn't remember having a single adulterous thought in his entire adult life. But he couldn't forget that kiss.

He landed out by the pool—thankfully *not* destroying the waterfall slide this time—but no one came out to meet him. In fact, the house seemed unusually quiet, for all that his wife and two teenage children were ostensibly inside. Mike should have been playing his guitar in the garage, or Chuck should have been killing zombies in a really loud video game in the private screening room. Instead, all was silent, and aside from lights on in the kitchen, the cabin was dark.

Unease settled over Jaccob's shoulders, and his armor suddenly felt stifling. "Computer," he said, voice cracking, "activate lifescanner."

Her hesitation actively grated on him this time, but only because he was nervous. "Four humanoid lifesigns in the house, Jaccob."

"Four?" He and Liz only had the two kids, so unless she hadn't told him about another one on the way (unlikely) or one of the existing kids had multiplied by mitosis (slightly more likely, but still improbable) then there was someone in his house who shouldn't be there. "Activate targeting computer."

"Are you sure, Jaccob?" the Computer asked. "More data processing—"

"Just activate it. Main screen."

The cheery, modern cabin faded in his view into a structured blueprint map as his sensors went to infrared. Colors bled away, leaving only a maze of blues and blacks, with two warm female bodies in the kitchen, next to a roaring oven. One of them had a knife and was pointing it at the other.

That was it.

Jaccob, the COO of a vast tech company taking a joyride in a sophisticated flying apparatus, vanished in the surge of fear. Stardust, hero of Cobalt City stood there instead.

"Combat mode," he said, and kicked the door off its hinges.

He strode into the dining room, his gauntlets humming and ready.

Liz leaned against the counter, her apron spattered with red liquid. His beautiful blonde wife looked startled. Lady Vengeance stood in front of her, holding a bottle of twenty-five-year-old scotch in one hand and a red-smeared knife in the other.

"Hi," she said, raising the knife to wave. "Don't freak out."

~

The wall exploded, sending a whirlwind of glass shards and twisted metal cascading into the pool. In the midst of the avalanche, Vivienne tumbled, shimmering with black and purple fear energy. She'd managed to conjure armor out of Stardust's extremely powerful fear to avoid being killed, but no one had hit her that hard in a long time. She splashed down into the pool, the cold water of which snapped her back into gasping reality in a rush. She thrashed, trying to right herself.

"What did I *just* say?" she shouted.

Stardust leaped out of the cabin, boot-jets humming as he hovered over the pool. His Starbolt blasters shrieked with power, ready to discharge right in her face. However much fear armor she mustered, there was no way she could stop that. Vivienne didn't even need to see his wide eyes through the visor to know he was furious. She could feel his emotions, which had turned from mostly fear to mostly anger.

"My family?" Stardust grabbed her by the collar of her drenched leather jacket and hoisted her into the air. "You came after—"

"Excuse me," said Liz Stevens from the blown-open cabin. She wiped at the tomato sauce smeared on her apron. "Honey, if you're quite finished blasting our dinner guest through walls, could you give me a hand chopping the carrots?"

Stardust looked to his uninjured wife, then back to Vivienne, then back. His gaze fell also on Michael and Charlotte, who peeped out from around the stairs.

"Uh," he said. "I thought—Liz, uh, I thought—"

Liz's demeanor turned icy. "Jaccob Drew Stevens, you put that woman down right now."

"Drew?" Vivienne murmured. "As in Andrew?"

"On its own actually," Stardust said, "and yes, dear!" He put Vivienne back on the porch and put his arms out to hug Liz. "I'm so glad you're—"

"Fine, thanks." Liz stepped past him toward her guest. "Are you all right?"

Vivienne accepted her hand and got up, albeit a little woozily. "That hurt a little, but he was scared enough I could take it."

"Good." Liz glanced back at Stardust over her shoulder. "He's a big softie, really."

"I'll take your word for it," Vivienne replied.

"It's actually a little reassuring he was scared for us," Liz said. "At least he didn't just wig out and attack you for no reason. He does that sometimes, you know."

"I know, right?" Vivienne headed back into the house with her. "Men."

"Seriously."

Stardust stood on the porch, totally confused. "Wait. What?"

~

Twenty minutes later, as the Stevens family sat down to lasagna and salad, their black-haired guest Lady Vengeance—Vivienne Cain—shared her story.

She told them how she'd been on the run from the Raven as far away as Colorado but escaped through a matter transference teleporter. Upon arriving in Cobalt City, she'd called the emergency number on a business card she had from a kid named Marcus Castile, which she'd obtained during events that lined up with his report. Stardust had showed up, she'd escaped with her malfunctioning powers, and bandaged up her wounds. He knew the rest, at least up until the police station. Later, Vivienne had gone to an internet lounge and googled "Stardust," which led to a link to Jaccob Stevens. This had in turn led her to the corporate headquarters of Starcom.

"It really wasn't hard to find you," Vivienne said. "That tower's pretty big."

Liz cleared her throat but said nothing.

"That and the Spirit guided me," Vivienne said.

"Spirit? You mean the Computer. Did she have a sexy, sort of British accent?"

Vivienne looked uncertain how to explain, and finally she shook her head. "Never mind."

"So ... you just came to the office?" Jaccob asked.

"I figured that was the only safe place to go, until I could get out of the city. After all, you saw how hard the Raven was trying to kill me, and you didn't let him. Thanks."

"No problem."

"So—" Jaccob checked out her not-bloody stomach. "You 100% now?"

"More or less. The nanobots did their job, and they're flushed out of my system."

"Isn't that a bad thing?"

"Not really. If they kept building new tissue, it would be the opposite of helping." Vivienne poured herself a fourth glass of wine. "I'm medicating."

Chuck and Mike were both at the dinner table, staring at Vivienne, who glanced at them every so often. They always looked away, but not fast enough. Mike was looking at her in shy adoration, like a student checking out his hot teacher, and he looked particularly embarrassed to be caught. Chuck's expression was a little more ambiguous: something not unlike admiration. He'd seen her look at only one other person that way: Kara Sparx,

Chuck's favorite superhero. Jaccob hoped Chuck didn't take too many cues from Vivienne—particularly the alcohol guzzling part.

"Anyway," Vivienne continued. "I went to your tower and tried to set up an appointment, but you were out at the moment. Fortunately, your wife here had stopped by to do some work while you were jetting around looking for me."

"Honey!" Jaccob said. "Danger!"

Liz sighed. "Jaccob, dear, Starcom Tower is the most secure place available other than the cabin. I just wanted to check on your projects. You know how you get when you're on a chase. Pass the salad, please."

"Anyway," Vivienne said. "After a momentary misunderstanding involving fear powers, we got to talking, then coffee, and then she invited me out here to crash and wait for the whole thing to blow over. Your couch is *so* comfy."

"Got to talking? Coffee? Then—?" Jaccob looked at Liz. "When did this even happen?"

"Focus, dear."

Vivienne had apparently been staying here ever since, which Liz hadn't told him about on the phone or in email, because the Raven could be tapping that. Liz hadn't expected Jaccob home for a couple more days—she knew him well enough to know he'd have to get some hero-ing out of his system.

"I didn't expect you to blow up half the house, though," she said.

"Sorry," Jaccob said. "So why is he after you? The Raven, I mean." Silence descended around the table, and everyone stared at Jaccob. "What'd I say?"

"I'll get some more wine," Liz said. "Everyone under twenty-one, time for bed."

"No way!" said Chuck, even as Mike whined, "aww, *Mom*!"

Liz shook her head firmly. "Would you go help them, dear?"

Since the kids were teenagers fully capable of putting themselves to bed, Jaccob understood this to be code for "make sure they're in bed." He did so, suggesting warm milk, tuck-ins, bedtime stories, etc., until he embarrassed the kids to their rooms. Parents needed to master many different weapons to prod their kids into doing something, and Jaccob had always wielded embarrassment like a savant.

Chuck shut her door tight, and Jaccob respected her "intruders will be sacrificed to Cthulhu" sign. Instead, he tapped on Mike's door. "Everything all right?"

Mike had decorated his room at the cabin with posters of the various rock bands he was into, and it was a fair-sized junkyard of musical instruments and sound equipment. With Mike's rock star aspirations, Jaccob and Liz usually had to ask him several times a night to stop playing so they could sleep. Not so tonight. The boy was sitting in bed, staring down at the floor as though he could see the dining room below. Spread out on the bed before him were half a dozen slightly-yellowed comic books, adorned with heroic images of spandex-clad figures of impossible proportions.

"That's her, isn't it?" Jaccob pointed to the cover of a trade comic book called *Lady Vengeance: Fallen Angel*. "Wow, that—that art is really exaggerated."

"Um, not *that* much."

"You need a girlfriend, don't you?" said Jaccob.

Mike looked even more embarrassed than before and stacked up the comics to hide them away. "Had a lot of girlfriends, did you Dad?"

"Yeah," he said. "They were all your mother."

Usually the idea of romance between his parents was an excellent way to distract Mike, but he seemed unfazed. "I didn't mean to stare at her like that. She's just ... she's just such a MILF."

"MILF?" Jaccob frowned.

"Jeez, Dad—never mind," Mike said. "You're, uh, you're not cheating on Mom with Lady Vengeance, are you?"

"What?" Jaccob did a second take. "No, of course not! Why would you even ask something like that? Your mother and I—"

"Good," Mike said. "'Cuz Mom would totally beat the living shit out of you."

"Definitely." Jaccob smiled. "And don't say 'shit.' "

He closed the door and headed back down to the living room, where the ladies had moved. Liz had brought over a fresh wine bottle and three glasses, but Vivienne looked content to curl up with the scotch. Wearing her silvery claw, she looked like an alcoholic mama bear. Jaccob came in at the end of a joke he didn't get at which Liz laughed and Vivienne gave her a wicked sort of smile. It looked almost peaceful, the two women who hadn't known each other more than a couple days lounging around like old friends. They immediately got serious when they saw him, however.

"So what's the big deal?" Jaccob asked. "It can't be that bad."

Liz fixed him with a warning look, but Vivienne waved her concern away.

"It's pretty simple," she said, clicking her claw absently. "The Raven is convinced I'm a super-villain in disguise, possessed by a devil to enhance my powers, and I'm apt to take over the whole world if I have a bad day. Oh, and I'm behind the murder of most of our friends, which he escaped, only losing an eye. Which I gouged out of his head."

Jaccob and Liz stared wordlessly. Vivienne took a swig of scotch and inspected the bottle's label for a few seconds.

"Trouble is," Vivienne said, "he's sort of got a point."

~

Having just finished reviewing the technical schematics of Jaccob Stevens' cabin by the lake, the Raven set his tea on Jaccob Stevens' desk and finally sank back in his chair. The digital clock played a jaunty spaceman tune, announcing 10 p.m. That knockout drug would be wearing off soon, so he thought he should go take care of Marjorie. But first ... His radar announced a vehicle landing on the roof, and he made sure the defenses were deactivated.

The girls were here.

He went out to meet them: H with her folded titanium-vanadium katana, M with her assault carbines. "*Capitán*," they said at the same time.

He showed them his tablet, in which they saw a live feed of Lady Vengeance and Liz Stevens at a table, talking. The feed was coming through the camera he'd imbedded in the stealth tech, which of course Jaccob had installed on the Stardust armor. The Raven had been watching them for hours and knew exactly how to proceed.

"We have work to do," he said. "Get ready."

CHAPTER NINE

WHAT EVERY MAN FEARS

"Mrff."

The first thing Vivienne did when she opened her eyes was to pop two stolen Vicodin from the bedside table and chase them down with a swig of whiskey. The second thing was to pat the empty bed beside her and sigh.

"Probably for the best," she murmured.

Vivienne snuggled deeper under the pillows for a minute or two. She hoped she'd fall back asleep, but the daylight in the room kept the drugs from kicking in. That or the raging hangover. She hadn't filched enough whiskey from the pantry to drink that away.

"Damn." One of the many problems of latent alcoholism was a high tolerance.

The crispy tang of bacon aroused her nose.

"Well, there's always that."

~

"Hungry, honey?"

"Hmm?" Jaccob looked up at his wife. "Uh no, not really."

"Suit yourself." Liz poured orange juice for the kids and coffee for herself, then headed back into the kitchen. She hummed something uplifting to herself.

Both the Stevens men seemed to have left their appetites at dinner the previous evening. Mike stared out the window, looking just as dreamy as Jaccob felt. Chuck ate enough for all of them, though, scarfing down waffles like it was going out of style. She neglected the bacon, though—she'd been vegan since fifth grade.

His mind drifted back to the night before. No matter how hard he tried, he simply could not stop thinking about what Lady Vengeance had told them the previous night. Her powers, she explained, were empathic in nature, but they didn't pick up the emotions of just humans. Rather, she was open to considerably more powerful, darker entities, including ...

~

"Azazel," Vivienne said, and Jaccob swore he felt a cold draft. "The devil constantly wants me to let go and surrender my body and powers to him. This—" Vivienne waved the scotch bottle around, and almost dropped it on the table. She was really drunk. "This drowns him out. Mostly."

"The devil doesn't exist." Even as he said it, Jaccob shivered.

"So you say," she said. "It was when I first joined Supergroup—along with the Raven, though he was only the old Raven's sidekick at the time. I was sixteen and stupid. My powers had manifested years earlier, but that ... *he* was my first. Which complicated everything."

"Azazel, you mean?" Jaccob asked. "There's more than one devil?"

Liz shushed him. The two women seemed to share a certain understanding to which he was not party. There was something between them, too. They sparked.

Jaccob settled back in his seat.

"Anyway," she said. "Azazel took me over. I've never been as powerful as I was for those few days—or as afraid. Supergroup stopped me, including the second Raven. They defeated the demon but didn't expunge it. He's always been there."

"He's taken you over other times?" Liz asked.

Lady Vengeance drank deep. "Maybe."

"What do you mean *maybe*?" Jaccob asked. "You don't know?"

"Jaccob! Don't badger her," Liz said. "That's enough for tonight. It's been a long day, and we could all use some rest."

Vivienne only shook her head and looked sick. Liz took her to the bathroom, and Jaccob heard them whispering, along with the occasional sound of weeping or vomiting.

He stood outside the door for a while, hand raised, but he never quite mustered the courage to interrupt. When Liz came out, she gave him a tired look and said she was going to bed. If he didn't know better, he'd have thought she was blushing.

He knocked on the bathroom door, which swung open slightly. He saw Vivienne looking at herself in the mirror. She looked pale and vulnerable and very, very tired. She was also disrobing to get into the shower.

"Hey," he said, then realized she was half-naked. "Sorry, I didn't mean—"

She gave him a look, then reached back and shut the door.

~

Jaccob was still wondering about it now, the following morning. What Vivienne had said, what Mike had said about her, that little flash of more than a married man was supposed to see ... He just couldn't get those things out of his head.

Shuffling footsteps drew his attention to the stairs, where Vivienne was limping down, looking strung out and not at all like a demon-possessed witch. She wore black sweatpants with a camisole that said "I heart Capes" and had serious bedhead. Based on the way Mike was staring at her, open-mouthed, Jaccob wasn't the only one who thought it was a good look.

"Good, uh, good morning," he said, tripping over himself at the awkwardness.

Vivienne totally ignored him. "Oh my god, coffee," she said, or something to that effect. She slumped down in Liz's empty chair and claimed her mug.

"That's mom's seat," Chuck pointed out.

"Uh huh." Vivienne pulled a mostly-empty bottle of whisky from her pocket and poured a generous dose into the coffee.

"No time for breakfast this morning," Liz said. "I've got to go in to the office early."

Cries of protest rang out around the table.

"What? It's not safe!" Jaccob said.

"Can't Dad go?" Chuck said.

Mike stared at Vivienne, completely ignoring everyone else.

"Nonsense, honey," Liz said. "And no, Charlotte, your dad can't go because he has to stay here and protect our guest from the people who are after her." She headed into the kitchen.

"Protect *us* from *her*, is more like it," Chuck said under her breath.

Huh. Maybe Jaccob had misread his daughter's feelings toward Vivienne. That sounded pretty hostile.

Vivienne sipped her boozed-up coffee, seemingly oblivious to the conversation.

Jaccob joined Liz in the kitchen where she was putting together the kids' lunches. There was no school today, but the ritual had become a shared habit of theirs—and inevitably the kids would take a drive somewhere today. Mike took the car out every chance he got. Jaccob set out the carrots to chop, but anxiety stopped him.

"Are you sure about this?" he asked.

"Of course." Liz took over slicing the carrots with vigorous, quick cuts. "This Raven person only wants Vee, after all."

"'Vee'?" Jaccob smirked. "I guess you're getting along really well."

"Anyway." Liz looked away. "He's not going to risk going to war with you—with Starcom—by attacking me. It's far more likely he's going to attack the cabin, once he figures out she's here. And besides, I'll have the Computer to protect me at the tower."

"That's—that's not what I meant."

The knife slipped, and Liz winced and drew her hand back. Blood welled up from a tiny cut in her index finger. Jaccob reached for her hand, but Liz pulled away and put her finger in her mouth. "You're worried about me leaving you alone with her?"

Jaccob understood that tone. "No—nothing like that," he said. "I only meant about Lady Vengeance going all demony on us. You heard what she said last night."

"I did, and I trust her." Liz sucked on her wound. "And I trust you too. Or should I be worried? I mean, you always were a sucker for damsels in distress."

"Hey." Jaccob took Liz's hand and kissed the cut on her finger. "You don't even need to ask me that. Besides, I'd never get past Mike."

They both leaned over to look out into the dining room, where Chuck sullenly glared out the window, Vivienne focused on her breakfast, and Mike mooned over her like a puppy.

"More, uh—more bacon?" Mike asked.

"Thanks, kid." Vivienne flashed him a friendly, dismissive smile.

Mike blushed.

"It's really pretty adorable," Liz said.

"I know, right?" Jaccob beamed. "Last night he called her something stupid cute. Like an elf or something. What was it? A 'melf?"

"MILF?" Liz's smile drained away.

"That was it," Jaccob said. "What's—?"

"I'll tell you later." She cleared her throat. "*Mike*! Go to your room!"

Their son bolted up, looking startled. "But—I didn't do anything!"

"*Now*."

"Tough break, kid," Vivienne said. "Better listen to your mom."

"Man!" Mike took a moment to compose himself, then stomped up the stairs.

"Remind me never to say anything to piss you off," Jaccob said.

"Every day." Liz was still watching the stairs. "Did he say anything else about her I should know about?"

What Mike *had* said—asking Jaccob if he was cheating on his wife—would fit both those categories. And while he and his wife tried to keep no secrets from each other, this one seemed inappropriate to share just then.

"You're at least going to take the jeep, right?" Jaccob asked. "With the upgraded defense systems? And the stinger missiles?"

"Fine. Be good."

"You too."

They shared a relaxed kiss, and Liz left Jaccob standing in the kitchen. He finished up the kids' lunches and stuck them in the fridge. The door felt heavy.

Back in the dining room, Chuck was enraptured in a story Vivienne was telling. Apparently, the coffee/whisky mixture livened their guest up, and without Mike in the room, Chuck had abandoned the sullen routine. "So then this complete douche nozzle says, with a straight face, 'It's E = MC squared. You know? Like the equation? You get it!' And I'm trying not to laugh because all I can think is, 'fuck, you have a *real* name?'"

Chuck laughed uproariously.

"Ladies! Language!" Jaccob said.

"C'mon, Dad!" Chuck's eyes were bright. "What happened then?"

"I said it, of course." Vivienne smiled. "Then I cut his arm in half with my claw. Don't worry—it was a robot arm. At least, I think so."

Again, Chuck laughed.

Jaccob was about to intercede when the alert on his HUD blinked to life. Chuck went instantly serious—she knew what that meant.

"That looks grim." Vivienne polished off the last of her spiked coffee.

"Perimeter breach," Jaccob said.

"Mom just left!" Chuck said.

Jaccob shook his head. "The signal is coming from the opposite end of the compound, four miles from the road. It's probably just a lost hiker. I'll go check it out."

"I'll come too." Vivienne rose from the table, a little woozy.

"No, that's ok," Jaccob said. "I can handle it."

"Hey, you know the area, but I know the Raven," she said. "Maybe I'll see something you don't."

Jaccob wasn't sure about that idea, but he couldn't argue with the practicality. "Fine, but it's a little chilly out there. You should probably get dressed."

"I'll get the tights."

"If you want. Also, use this." He handed her a gadget the size of a cellphone.

"Not really a portable electronics kind of girl," she said.

Jaccob pushed a button, and the light bent around Vivienne, projecting a holographic image. Her hair turned blonde, her skin tanned, her figure slimmed slightly. She became an entirely different person: Liz, actually.

"OK, that's cool," she said. "A blonde, though? Blondes never do it for me."

Chuck cast Jaccob an accusatory look, which he did his best to ignore.

"Let's go," he said. "I'll fly."

~

With the wind whipping through her unfortunately blond hair, Vivienne had to admit that the image inducer thingamabob was pretty neat. She didn't *feel* any different, but for all intents and purposes, so long as she held the projector, she became a different person. It reminded her of using her powers to take on the aspect of an opponent's worst fear. The tech wasn't as effective as the magic, perhaps, but it required a lot less effort. Such a handy little device.

It was also revealing, in a psychological way that she was trying and failing to ignore. Ultimately, she had to ask.

"Jaccob," she said, but the wind tore away her voice.

She hated flying, particularly when it involved being carried by someone with environmental conditioning *inside* his suit. She'd had all sorts of aches and bruises when they landed, and it was *freezing* even at this low altitude. How Stardust managed to talk anyone into piggy-backing on his power armor was beyond her. She shut her eyes and held on a little tighter.

After sixty-eight uncomfortable seconds, Stardust set down near the edge of his property off in the woods. The area was gorgeous from a natural standpoint: old growth trees that formed a natural faerie circle filled with flowers. From here, she could dimly see the distant skyline of Cobalt City through gray clouds. Good thing she'd taken his advice and put on jeans and a coat, or she'd be half frozen by now.

"That was fun," she said, shivering a little. "Only almost passed out once."

Stardust ignored her and swept the area, which made a beam of light play across his visor like a scanner. "This is where the sensor was tripped, but there's nothing unusual," he said. "No tracks, heat signatures, nothing. Did it just malfunction?"

"Could be." Vivienne leaned against a tree and twisted a lock of curly blond hair between her fingers. "Can I ask you a question, Jaccob?"

"I prefer Stardust when I'm in the armor, Lady Vengeance."

"OK, *Jaccob*," she said. "So what's with making me look like your wife? And don't pretend it's a coincidence. Chuck totally picked up on it."

His helmet hid his eyes, so she could only see half his expression in response to that—a quivering jaw that spoke of discomfort. "If the Raven is watching right now, you have to be someone he expects to be here."

"You do this often?" Vivienne asked. "Just whisk your wife away in your arms to some romantic forest grove on your private estate?"

Now he smiled slightly. "More often than you'd think."

"I *knew* it." Vivienne looked around the grove. "What if he's listening in, though? Hearing me talk about myself in the third person?"

"If he can breach my armor's jamming tech, he deserves to catch us," Stardust explained. "Starcom is, after all, the world's leader in static and dropped calls. Not that I'll ever admit it at the annual shareholders' conference."

"Question still stands," Vivienne said. "What's up with making me look like your wife? I mean, I get it, she's really hot, but this is going to get weird, isn't it?"

"It's already a little bit weird." Stardust crossed his arms. "You come out of nowhere, attack me, kidnap my wife, crash at my house, and what, now we're allies against the Raven?"

"Technically you attacked *me*, but otherwise—yeah, pretty much."

"Only because you were endangering the city with your crazy fear powers."

"Trust me, Sparky," Vivienne said. "If I were endangering the city, you'd know."

"Like you did with Azazel?" Stardust asked. "Exactly how powerful are you?"

"I can't really explain it in a way your scientific brain would understand."

"That powerful, huh?" Stardust said. "And how exactly am I supposed to know if you're being taken over by a devil and running amok? You know, if we get in a battle and it's either you or the end of the world. How do I know what that'll be like?"

"You don't." She stretched. "But come on. You know you want to."

"Do I?" Stardust stood his ground.

"Sure you do." Vivienne counted off the reasons on her fingers, coming a step closer each time. "Of all the Protectorate, you're the only one who still puts on the cape and goes out to fight crime. You have this giant obelisk in the middle of Cobalt City bristling with high-tech toys and evil-smiting gadgets. Your first reaction to super-people you don't know coming to your city is to head straight for the power armor. And you're not getting any younger." Now she was right in his face. "What drives you, except *want*? To know, to experience ... What else is there?"

Stardust looked down at her. "You mean besides the cool suit?"

Vivienne couldn't help but smile. "You just never want to grow up, do you?"

"Deathly terrified of it," Stardust said. "Can't you tell? With your fear thingy?"

He was like a dog staring at a bone—she couldn't distract his attention from the point. Her powers scared him, and he needed to understand them.

Good luck.

"Well," she said, "I can tell you're a deeply insecure man, with all kinds of fears. The kind of man I could wrap around my finger with my powers. Hmm." She touched his arm. "I'm thinking about it."

She expected him to blush uncomfortably and retreat—she was trying to make him do that, after all—but instead he puffed up and met her gaze without flinching.

"Fear thingy me," he said.

"What, really?"

"Totally." He stood tall.

Vivienne was unconvinced. "You really want me to do this?"

Stardust nodded. "You fear thingied me a couple times before, and I fought my way free. I need to figure it out. If the worst-case scenario should happen, and I need to take you down."

"The worst-case scenario?" Vivienne smiled wanly. "You mean, if I get possessed by Azazel, and you need to kill me for the good of the world?"

"Exactly like that."

"You're cute when you're all earnest. I can see what Liz sees in you." She shook her head. "It's not going to do any good against Azazel. Thirty years ago, he made me so powerful I could crush Supergroup without trying. I could just look at a man, and he'd bow to my will. And I'm a lot older and better at my powers now."

"Not *that* much older."

"Aww." He probably thought that was a compliment. "Fuck it. If it'll make you feel better, let's do this." Vivienne laid her hands on his cheeks and reached out with her power to draw on Stardust's fear. "Here goes."

She reached out tentatively, but with growing certainty, feeling the flow of Stardust's feelings. It wasn't difficult—he wore his feelings like a summer jacket, right there for her to tap.

He shivered. "This is going to hurt, isn't it?"

"It'll feel a little weird, but it won't hurt," Vivienne said. "At least, not much."

Stardust sighed. "I hate magic."

"And I hate shaving my legs, but we all have our crosses to bear."

His power armor provided no protection against her powers, though he was obviously much more confident wearing it than not. Confidence made it hard to get a handle on his fears, but she pressed deeper. Once she had worked out his darkest fear, she could use it against him.

She expected to have to work at it for a while, but from the first time she had used her powers on him, his fear had been unveiled to her. It was all bound up in feelings of inadequacy and needing to be loved, but once she pushed past the distractions, she found the heart of it. And it was much as she suspected—and feared.

She let go of his face and pulled away as though from a red-hot burner. They were standing close enough to kiss, and that wasn't where she wanted to be just then.

"Was that it?" Stardust looked startled. "You didn't even do your thingy on me. I mean, I assume, because no buildings hit me with other buildings this time."

Vivienne shook her head, fighting down a wave of nausea. "You're pretty strong," she said. "You'll be fine. You know, if I go crazy and blow up the world and stuff. Can we go back now? I'm starting to lose my buzz, and you wouldn't like me when I'm sober."

"Are you all right?" Stardust reached for her, but she recoiled.

"Let's just go."

He hesitated, looking at her curiously.

"What."

"That thing you said, about my wife being hot."

"Oh my God," she said. "Yes, your wife is hot. Yes, I'm bisexual. Yes, I'd sleep with her. No, you can't watch."

"Bwuh." To his credit, Stardust's cheeks reddened through the visor. "But—I wasn't going to—I mean, that wasn't what I—?"

Seriously? Blushing? Adorable.

Vivienne looked away so he wouldn't see her smile. She actually felt a little better. But she still needed a drink. "Let's go."

~

Some ways off, the Raven watched the unfolding drama through his scope, thinking. Getting in had been difficult, and he did not dare try and disrupt the border defenses unnecessarily. Tipping his hand was not the way the Raven played the game. He moved only when he could not lose.

"*¿Es ella?*" H asked. "*¿Es Señora Cain?*"

"*Es Señora Stevens, claro,*" M said. "*Los dos están casi besando. Stardust no tiene deseo por Cain.*"

H glared at her partner. "*¡Cállate, tonto!*"

"*Silencio, vos.*" The Raven turned his scope slightly, then nodded. "It is Cain. She has a device that disguises her identity."

"*¿Verdad?*" H and M looked confused.

The Raven nodded and refocused his scope, which framed the real Liz Stevens, who had secreted herself behind a tree at the edge of the clearing. She'd left for the office, then must have turned back to get something she forgot. Of course, the tracking software was active in her jeep, so she'd known where to find Stardust. She'd seen the intimacy between Lady Vengeance as well as the Raven and his henchwomen had.

"This is how we do this," he said. "Listen."

PART THREE

SHELL GAME

CHAPTER TEN

HOSTILE TAKEOVER

That afternoon, Stardust jetted around the Skymall, cloaked, his mind roiling. He watched his radar carefully, locked onto the two female forms shopping in Nordstrom: his wife Liz and Vivienne. The two just clicked, for whatever reason, and interacted now as if they'd known each other for years. The two got along so well, Stardust could almost forget one of them was *Lady Vengeance.* Or that he kept thinking about her.

Or both of them.

He shook his head. "Stop that," he said under his breath.

Over his career, Stardust had met his fair share of hot heroines and smoldering villainesses, but he'd never given them much thought, if he'd even noticed. Maiden China, for instance, had carried a torch for him for years, going so far as to invade Cobalt City on a fleet of giant rubber duckies to visit him one Christmas. Silver Mantis had taken a break from her plan for ultimate insectile domination to flirt with him and try to bite his head off. Stiletto had taken the fact that her blades couldn't pierce his armor as a sign they were meant to be together. Heck, the hell queen Darla Spider had used dark magic to merge her company with Starcom—no innuendo there.

He'd found these all flattering and sometimes inconvenient, but that was it. No evil temptresses or sexy power-women had so much as turned his head. Liz had always been more than enough. But Vivienne ... She was obviously very attractive and age-appropriate. And while she seemed uninterested, he couldn't stop thinking about her.

Maybe it wasn't actually her, but what she represented: a way to get back in the saddle. After all, if *she* could still be a hero past forty, why couldn't *he*?

"I'm having a damn mid-life crisis," he grumbled.

After one of their rare arguments, Liz had talked him into letting them go back to Cobalt City to shop for some fresh clothes for Vivienne—so she wouldn't just keep borrowing Liz's—on the condition that he escort them, fully armored. With an image projector (based on an invention Kara Sparx had made for Snowflake back in the Protectorate days), Vivienne looked like a pretty redhead. The default image was blonde, but he'd made the adjustment at her request.

"And no sneaky blasting her with a Starbolt and arresting her," Liz had added.

"Yes, dear," he had said, with a touch of resentment.

He hadn't told her about the forest, and she hadn't asked.

Fast forward a few hours, and he found himself floating around the Skymall, looking in all directions and hoping to see the Raven before he struck. He checked the stealth tech, which seemed to be functioning normally. As he hovered around the mall, he couldn't see himself in the big shiny windows. He tested it a few times, zipping by at various speeds so he could check for a reflection. So cool.

He'd felt so restless lately—itching for a fight. He only now realized that his family had somehow made him feel constricted for quite some time. Would another guy in his situation be out buying an expensive sports car or running around with an entourage of strippers? Maybe he just needed to build a new suit. One with wings.

Couldn't the ladies hurry it up? They'd been shopping about an hour now, and all seemed fine. No sign of the Raven or anything weird on the radar, but how long would that last?

"Hurry up," he said irritably. "What could possibly be taking so long?"

~

"You think he's figured it out yet?" Vivienne asked.

"That this whole plan is to lure the Raven out of hiding so they can fight?" Liz asked. "Let it be a pleasant surprise."

Vivienne nodded, impressed. In contrast to her earnest and forthright husband, Elizabeth Stevens had proved herself calculating and demonstrated a certain amount of ruthlessness. Manipulating Jaccob as Stardust to take down the Raven scored points in Vivienne's book.

"You know what would look great on you?" Liz asked. "These."

She held up a pair of red pumps that were both stylish and, admittedly, very cute. They were also on the order of $900.

"Do they have them in black?" Vivienne asked. "No? What a shame."

Liz would not be deterred. "You really should expand your color palette."

"I like what I like. But ok, I'll try them." Vivienne consented to trying the shoes, which looked amazing and pinched only a little.

They'd been shopping all day, hitting fancy boutique after designer outlet. Vivienne had agreed to let Liz buy her some new clothes, but Liz's taste in clothes ran to the extravagant. Simply not used to having so much bank lavished upon her, Vivienne had finally bargained Liz down to Nordstrom, after the woman adamantly refused to go into any of the bigger department stores.

"I'm so glad we got to do this," Liz said. "Since Charlotte turned thirteen and began her ridiculous obsession with combat boots and leather jackets, it's not often I get the chance to buy anything designed by an actual designer."

For Vivienne—who had worn her fair share of biker gear in her life—the heels were awkward, but she did like them. "They're cute, but the bar doesn't pay that well."

"My treat," Liz said. "No objections."

"Are you for real?" Vivienne asked. "You're just going to drop a thousand bucks on a random stranger?"

"You're not—" Liz smiled. "Starcom pays its CEO ridiculously well, and who do you think built that company? Certainly not Jaccob."

"No doubt," Vivienne said. "But heels just aren't my style. Thanks, though."

Liz shrugged. "Can't blame a lady for trying, even if I could tell when we first met you were all about the boots."

"The tights gave it away, huh?" Vivienne fidgeted, her hands shaking a little as the haze of drinking all morning started to fade. "Your husband seems ... very nice."

"He is." Liz smiled and put her hand on Vivienne's arm. "But no more about Jaccob, all right? We're two self-actualized women out on the town. The last thing we want to talk about is *men*."

"Heh." Not that it was going to stop Vivienne *thinking* about men—one in particular. This whole shopping trip was dangerous with the Raven out there unaccounted for, but Liz hardly seemed worried. Did she just not understand the risks?

"I should probably check on the kids." Liz pulled out her phone. "They weren't happy they had to stay home during Spring Break, so who knows what they're up to?"

To Vivienne, it was obvious what Liz was doing, from opening her home to replacing Vivienne's wardrobe to setting up this little ambush for the Raven. Liz was the sort of person who saw someone in need and just had to help. She was like Jaccob in that way, albeit actually subtle. She could actually make Vivienne relax, and even laugh a little. Vivienne liked the Stevens family—she really did. Still, she'd known her share of people like Liz and Jaccob, and knew they were the type who always got hurt the most, particularly around her.

Her only option at this point was to leave.

It was long past time to make good her escape. She could get money out of Liz and hop the next flight out of Cobalt City. Returning to Seattle seemed like a bad choice, unless she wanted to bring the Raven down on her friends or even her enemies in the city. Up until last week he'd thought her dead, so she'd been safe, but now ... Now her only option was to run and hide.

Maybe she should do it now, while Liz was distracted. Vivienne could trap her in her fear and guide her to the nearest ATM. It would be ungrateful and cruel, but Vivienne preferred Liz to think of her as a raging bitch than to be dead.

"So," Liz said suddenly while they were in the checkout line at Nordstrom. She'd just hung up the phone. "Did you do it?"

The question took Vivienne by surprise. "What?"

Liz slid the phone back into her bag. "Did you kill them?"

The realization crashed in: what Liz meant. She hadn't told Jaccob the story, but Liz had confronted her about it that first night. In a growing haze of liquor-buzz, Vivienne had told Liz the story of her bloody parting with the Raven the night Supergroup had died. How she'd managed to escape, then gone to the Raven, begging him to explain what was going on. How instead of helping, he'd attacked her as the traitor. After all, her fear powers would produce specters of villains that would vanish after a battle, and she was drunk out of her mind half the time. How was he to know the demon hadn't made her do it—that she wasn't the demon right then?

She wouldn't have escaped without Azazel to fight the Raven off. The battle had been ferocious, and he'd lost an eye in the bargain. Horrified, Vivienne had taken back over and stopped the fight, but the damage was done: the Raven lay unconscious and bleeding at her feet. She'd fled, because if she stayed any longer, Azazel would take her again and kill him. She remembered reading with relief that the Raven had survived.

He'd conquered Colorado and set up Valhalla a few years afterward, and she hadn't seen him since. Vivienne had never quite accepted that the Raven thought she was dead, but with all the liquor at the bar in Seattle, she'd managed to forget about him and his accusations—at least a little bit.

"So did you do it?" Liz asked again, her face set and her eyes full of resolve. "Jaccob isn't here. You can tell me."

Now they all came back. Liz had forcibly reminded Vivienne not just about the Raven, but also his horrible accusation that she had murdered Supergroup: friends, lovers, rivals—the only family Vivienne had ever known.

"I told you," Vivienne said, her words as frosty as though she'd opened a deep freezer rather than her mouth. "I told you what happened."

Darkness stirred inside her, her powers awakening and reaching out to the other customers. They all had small, insignificant fears compared to hers: they worried about picking up their kids from soccer practice, or whether they'd deleted their internet histories before their spouses got home, or if such and such politician would be better than another who made different promises but would do exactly the same thing. None of them had faced what Vivienne had—none of them had the slightest idea what real fear was. But Vivienne could see that when they looked at her, as the light drained from the air around her and her eyes filled with liquid blackness, they started to understand.

Show them, Azazel said in her head, remarkably clear despite the bottle of scotch she'd polished off the previous night. *Show them what to fear.*

No!

"What is this?" Vivienne said. "You think you let me crash on your couch, and it means you know me? You don't know me. You don't know half the shit I've done." She grew taller, her body filling out with terror. "You have no idea what I'm capable of."

Liz faced her directly, neither intimidated by her harsh words nor touched by her dark powers. She had fears, certainly—fears for her kids, fears for her husband, fears for her city—but none for herself. She pushed past her anxiety to confront her new friend—hopped up on fear or not—with the sort of take-no-crap attitude only mothers and the wives of superheroes could manage.

"What are you afraid of, Liz?" Vivienne reached toward her face. "It's only fair, if you're going to ask me that. Afraid for your precious tech empire? Your family?" Then, because it was awful of her: "Afraid I'm going to steal your husband, maybe?"

Liz recoiled at first, but when Vivienne mentioned Jaccob, she suddenly stood firm. "I saw you two in the forest. I'm not afraid of you."

Vivienne grinned, her teeth like knives. "You should be."

"But I'm not." Liz's throat worked. "We may have just met, but I know you're a good person. However much you try and hide it."

"I—" Vivienne hesitated, her powers at maximum, her fingers just an inch from Liz's face. Then she lowered her hand. She averted her eyes. "Goddammit."

"Vivienne," she said. "You can tell me."

"I don't—" Vivienne's mantle of fear shivered, and the darkness that had surrounded her cracked, then splintered. "I don't know, all right?"

The customers at Nordstrom breathed easier and looked around for the source of the strange chill. Liz took Vivienne by the arm and pulled her away behind a rack of shoes. "What do you mean you don't know?" Liz asked.

"I don't *remember.*" Tears leaked out Vivienne's eyes—salty, rather than black and toxic. "I was so drunk. You don't even know. It was a reunion with all those people who hated me or wanted to fuck me or both. Of course I was drunk. How—" She sniffed involuntarily. "How would I know?"

Liz looked at her a long, long time, and finally nodded. "You didn't do it."

"I didn't?" Vivienne was confused.

"You're self-destructive, self-loathing, and self-deceptive," Liz said. "But you aren't that person. You aren't a killer."

"How would you know?" Vivienne asked.

"I just do," Liz said. "This is about the Raven, isn't it? You hurt him, and you can't get over it. You guys were together, right?" She touched Vivienne's hand. "Believe me, I've been in enough bad relationships to recognize a thing with an ex when I see it."

"Huh," Vivienne said. "I'm sorry about the thing with Jaccob by the way."

"Hey, I understand," she said. "He's totally cute."

"Geeky cute."

Liz's cell phone rang a jaunty melody, and she picked up. "Hello?"

Vivienne could hear Jaccob's voice crackling loudly through the phone. "He's coming right at you. Hold on!"

~

The Raven watched from a distance through his scope. He could see, of course, through Stardust's visor, but the man kept looking at himself in the windows, rather than watching anything useful.

Through the zoom, he saw two women out shopping, one of which was Elizabeth Stevens, while he suspected the other was Vivienne Cain. She was cloaked in some sort of image projector, which he respected highly. He'd been working on just such a device for years but hadn't yet perfected it. The image inducer existed nowhere in Starcom's files, and the Raven suspected he hadn't built it himself. The style was all wrong—too few bells and whistles on the device, and too many random diodes.

"H, M," he said into his HUD. "¿Estan listos?"

"*Sí, capitán,*" they said, and clicked off.

The Raven prepared to move. "Computer, prepare for Operation Whiteout."

"Are you sure, The Raven?" asked the sexy voice. "That seems very dangerous. The chances of causing serious injury to Jaccob are—"

He ignored her protestations and started running. Of course he popped up on Stardust's radar—he had planned as much—and of course Stardust flickered into visibility and intercepted him as he leaped toward the Skymall. The armored hero hit him with a tackle from above, and the two plummeted toward the busy street.

The Raven heard Jaccob Stevens shouting into Stardust's communicator. "Liz, get back to the car! I'll handle this."

The Raven smiled.

~

"Jeez, Mom!" said Mike Stevens from the passenger seat. "Of course I haven't left the cabin. Thanks for checking on us like every five minutes. *God!*" He hung up.

"Was that Mom?" Chuck asked, arms out straight as she steered the Audi. She focused on the curving forest road, which was harder to see as evening fell.

"Yeah." Mike clicked through the windows on his phone. "Figures she wouldn't trust us to stay put. We're totally responsible."

"Totally!" Chuck took the next turn at eighty miles an hour—twice the speed limit.

"Lights, by the way. You always forget those."

"Yeah, yeah." Chuck flipped the lights on.

They cruised along at a ridiculous speed through the country roads, the way they usually did when both parents went into town and left them to their own devices. It was really quite amusing how their dad thought the security program on the Audi's ignition would keep them out. How else was Mike going to teach Chuck to drive?

"Woah, woah," Mike said. "Pull over."

"What?"

"Pull over!" Mike said, pointing.

A red Mustang sat by the side of the road, broken down and smoking. Chuck could tell where Mike was looking: the heart-shaped backside of a Latina girl bending over the engine. Another girl was waving them down.

"Careful," Chuck said. "They could be terrorists. Or super-villains. Or worse—groupies."

"That sounds totally awesome."

Chuck shook her head. "You sound just like Dad."

"And you sound just like Mom."

"I do not!"

Mike leaned out the window as they pulled up. "*¿Que pasa, chicas?*"

"Oh my God." Chuck reddened with embarrassment.

The girl who'd been waving came over, and the grease-monkey regarded them as she ran her hand through her hair. Both in their early twenties and gorgeous, they looked similar enough to be sisters. They didn't seem to speak much English, but their smiles were effective enough on the spellbound Mike.

"Woah, woah, not so fast," Mike said. "What are your names?"

The girls looked at one another, then giggled. "Havana," said the driver, and the grease monkey said, "Magdalena."

"It's like a dream come true," Mike was practically drooling.

"Just call a tow-truck," Chuck said. "*God.*"

"Oops, battery's low." Mike threw his phone out the window. "You need a ride?"

"You are such an idiot," Chuck said.

The Latinas shared an almost militaristic nod, then piled in.

CHAPTER ELEVEN

HOME INVASION

As Stardust and the Raven collided outside, an explosion of force ripped through downtown Cobalt City, rocking the Skymall to its foundations.

"I have to get out there," Vivienne said.

"No." Liz took her arm. "You're the one the Raven wants—if you join the fight, Jaccob will have to worry about protecting you as well as himself. It would defeat the whole purpose of this trap."

Vivienne watched out the window as Stardust and the Raven streamed past, the one strafing and blasting Starbolts, the other leaping back and forth between buildings like a cat. She looked down at her bare fingers, thinking of her claw, down in Liz's car. The Raven had built it with the same materials as his blades and taught her to use it.

"This doesn't seem right," Vivienne said as the two of them hurried down the concrete stairs to the level where they'd parked. "The Raven wouldn't do it like this. Come after us, sure, but he wouldn't just rush us. We're missing something."

"What are you thinking?" Liz asked.

"Call your kids," Vivienne said. "Make sure they're ok."

Liz's eyes widened, and she took the phone back out. She dialed, then shook her head. "Nothing. It went straight to voicemail."

"Call again." A familiar cold focus came over Vivienne, coupled with a sinking nausea in the pit of her stomach. She knew what was happening, though she could not quite say it. "And let's go."

Liz called five times with increasing anxiety as they hurried down to the parking garage. By the time they got to the car, her hands were shaking. "What's going on, V?" she asked. "What—?"

But she could see the flashing alarm on the dashboard as well as Vivienne could. She flicked on the audio, and Jaccob's sexy Computer said: "Proximity alert: non-Stevens intruders detected at Location: Cabin."

"But the Raven's out there," Liz said, trying to deny it. "Who could be—?"

"Groupies," Vivienne said. "Let's go."

Liz's rich-wife attitude evaporated, and she went full warrior-mom mode. "Get in."

She pushed a particular series of keys, and computers folded down into the Jeep's interior. "Command?" said the Computer, a little less relaxed than before.

"Flight mode," Liz said. "Permission November Alpha Tango Echo."

"Confirmed," said the Computer. The Jeep vibrated as it unfolded into an entirely different craft: one with wings and rockets.

"Flight mode?" Vivienne asked. "Of *course* it has a flight mode."

Liz nodded. "Hang on."

They zoomed back to the cabin, and Vivienne prayed they'd make it in time.

~

Stardust jolted the Raven out of his leap on the first pass, but after that, the fight immediately started going downhill—literally.

At first, they played cat and mouse. Stardust zipped around, sending Starbolt after Starbolt at the Raven, all of them on a rotating power modulation, so there was no way his armor could absorb them like before. The Raven found this out the hard way, when a bolt put him flat on his back—after that, he dodged and leaped from perch to perch like a panther. He didn't quite fly, exactly, but his enhanced boots and glider more than made up for it. Stardust kept strafing and blasting.

As difficult as the fight was, Stardust also found it exhilarating. He was a big-shot hero again, fighting a super-villain who had invaded this city—*his* city—and there was no way he was going to lose.

Not that it was easy. The Raven was so darned acrobatic that Stardust couldn't hit him manually, and his targeting system wasn't having much luck either. Was the Computer *trying* to make him miss?

"Computer!" he shouted, as the Raven rushed toward him. "Stop wasting time with your imaginary boyfriend and get your head in the game!"

"About that, Jaccob," the Computer said. "I have something to tell you."

"Like I said, call me Stardust when I'm in the armor," he said. "And can't it wait?"

The Raven grabbed Stardust and wrestled his boot-jets above them, so now they were flying straight down. As they went, the Raven caught Stardust in a headlock and ground his face against the side of the Skymall, loosing a shower of sparks and smoke behind them. Thank God he had the armor's forcefield up!

Stardust could not shake the relentless vigilante off, nor could he correct his course. He saw through a haze of sparks and grinding metal that the ground was approaching very quickly, and he had to do something—even if it was going to hurt.

"Yep," he said. "This is definitely going to hurt."

He put his hands to the Raven's chest and fired a concussive Starbolt blast. He had a split-second to savor the sight of the Raven being blown crazily away from him before the force slammed him the opposite direction, through a wall and into the parking structure of the Skymall. He took out two compact coupes and a minivan before he finally crashed to a halt against one of the support pillars.

He must have passed out for a while, because when he was next aware of the world, daylight was vanishing. The Raven lay on the roof of the building across the street, also stunned. As Stardust watched, the man shook his head and got to his feet.

The Computer spoke as Stardust sat there coughing. "Jaccob, your vital signs show increased stress, but there is no enemy combatant in range," she said. "Would now be a good time to talk? It's very important."

"No!" Stardust fired a Starbolt, but it hit nowhere near the Raven, who promptly vanished. "Damn it!"

A moment later, the Raven's single red eye appeared near the edge of the parking structure. Again, Stardust blasted, and again, he missed. The Raven ducked out of sight. Stupid targeting computer.

"Are you sure, Jaccob? It's pivotal."

The Raven appeared and came rushing at Stardust, blades scything forth. Stardust blasted them away and charged. "What is with you? Why can't—"

He was in mid-flight, soaring toward the Raven, when his armor powered off. Suddenly not a flying hero but instead four hundred pounds of dead weight, Jaccob crashed into a parked SUV, which promptly tipped, wobbled, and fell with a thunderous roar onto its side. He lay groaning on top of the felled vehicle, unable to move from the shock. What was going on? He'd dealt with the EMP issue, buffing up the Stardust armor shields. How ...?

The Raven crashed down on top of him, straddling Jaccob on the side of the overturned car. His helmet with its one red eye bent low as though sniffing at his fear.

"I have two suggestions for you, Jaccob Stevens," his thick voice crackled through the space between their helmets. "One, reconsider protecting her. You do not know how dangerous—"

"I know you're the one trying to murder her," Stardust said, "and that makes you the enemy." Why did the Raven's voice sound so familiar?

The Raven nodded, as if he had expected this answer. "Second, improve your security system."

"My security—what?"

Then he understood, as the Raven opened his helmet to reveal the face of Antonio Desantes, bereft of a left eye. It was just a yawning black socket.

Jaccob knew in an instant what had happened—how long had he been wearing the armor add-on that the Raven had given him? He'd given him access to Starcom, too!

That, and the Computer's buzzed voice: "I told you we needed to talk."

"Computer! How could you do this to me?" Jaccob asked.

"I'm sorry, Jaccob," she said. "He's just so darkly brilliant. Sometimes my motherboard just wants to be hacked like a 2-byte OS."

Jaccob sank back onto the dented SUV, panting. "If you're going to kill me, go ahead and do it," he said. "You've won, all right? You've won."

"Kill you? No." Antonio shook his head. "I don't want to hurt you or even defeat you. Just keep you here a little longer, and the girls will take care of the rest."

"*The girls*?" Jaccob's eyes widened. "Oh my God. What have you done?"

~

As they approached the cabin, Vivienne insisted that Liz land the jeep and drive up slowly. Flight mode was faster, but it made too much noise. Vivienne had also stopped Liz from calling the police or the Stevens' family private security. Sirens would tip off whatever the Raven had waiting just as surely as their car.

And what *was* waiting for them? The security report showed two foreign bodies at the cabin: two adults, it looked like, out back with the kids. Even if they were the twins—as she feared they might be—Vivienne thought she could handle them. She would have to, or they were all screwed.

By the time they pulled up, Liz was radiating enough fear and panic to make Vivienne dizzy. At the sight of the front door slightly ajar, Liz made a little moaning sound—like a wounded, rabid animal—and would have run to the cabin if Vivienne hadn't grabbed her arm. "I'll go," she said. "You stay in the car."

"Like hell!" Liz said.

"It's me they want," Vivienne said. "Not you, and not the children. If I let anything happen to you or the kids, your husband would throw me through another wall. So you stay in the car, where it's safe. Oh, and call the police. Now it's safe."

Liz stared at her, teeth grinding. "You don't know how this feels."

"Oh, I do. Believe me." Vivienne slurred her words with the heady taste of Liz's fear. She deactivated the image inducer and handed it to Liz. "If it's not me coming out of there, use this. Turn invisible or something. Do not take *any* risks."

"Shouldn't you take it?" Liz asked.

"It won't do any good," Vivienne said. "The Raven knows I'm here, and this is probably a trap, so there's no way I'm going to bluff my way through it. I need raw power, not trickery." She laid her fingers on Liz's face. "Do you trust me?"

Liz nodded.

Vivienne narrowed her eyes. "Then hang onto something."

She drank deep of Liz's fear for her kids, letting it flow into her and through her. She shaped the fear into black and purple armor that wrapped around her limbs. The talons of her claw—retrieved from the glove compartment—grew long and jagged. A long, slightly curved sword appeared under her other hand, and she took it by the hilt. She became a demonic samurai warrior, ready for all-out battle. Liz stared at her in fright—with good reason, considering that the armor came from her nightmares.

Without another word, Lady Vengeance headed in, clearing each room like a trained soldier. The kids' rooms were empty warzones. The kitchen was an absolute mess of spilled food. The 74-inch TV was blaring some music-video channel, which made her head ache. She sneaked through the cabin, the alternating lights casting strange shadows across her fearsword.

Lady Vengeance heard a sound from the back—a child's muffled cry—and went to investigate. She raised her sword.

Outside, the scene was idyllic. Chuck was sunbathing alongside a cute girl with golden skin and a black bikini with white spots. A girl who looked almost identical except for her own suit (white with black spots) swam in the pool, while Mike—looking very pleased with himself—looked on in obvious admiration. No one seemed to have noticed Lady Vengeance, and why would they, with the darkness bending to her will?

She consciously suppressed the effect, becoming merely herself. The power was still there, but this way she wouldn't terrify the kids when they saw her.

"Mike," she whispered, and saw the hairs rise on his neck. "Get out of here—right now. Take your sister and run to your mom."

Mike turned around, beaming. "Oh, hey, Ms. Cain," he said. "You should come join us! I'll bet mom has a spare suit—" An uncomfortable expression crossed his face, like he'd just imagined his mother in a bikini.

"No," Lady Vengeance said, "I mean, thanks I guess, but no—you have to leave. Like right fucking *now*—"

Then the girl swimming in the pool surfaced and brushed back her lustrous black hair. Her gleaming green eyes fell on Vivienne. "Target acquired."

"Target?" said Mike. "What—?"

The swimming girl leaped out of the pool, turned a cartwheel to her lawn chair, and drew a gleaming katana from the folded towel waiting there.

The kids' eyes went wide. "That—where did *that* come from?" Mike asked.

"Havana," Vivienne said to her, summoning her sword back into her hand. She looked at the other girl. "And Magdalena, too. Fantastic."

"What? What's going on?" Mike asked, stepping in the way. "I—"

"Mike!" Vivienne shouted. "Get behind me!"

"Lethal force authorized," said the other girl—the one lounging by Chuck.

She swept an automatic shotgun from under her chair and unloaded it at Vivienne—and at Mike, who stood stunned between them.

~

Jaccob was trapped. The Raven—Antonio—had taken away Stardust as surely as he'd just taken away his family.

"This is your own fault." Antonio grimaced. "You let that devil woman into your home—you let her eat your food, watch your children. Your biggest mistake was not in falling for my ruse, compromising your security, or even in facing me, but in trusting her. Believe me, I know." He rose up a little. "Sacrifices must be made to save the thousands that will die when Azazel takes hold of Lady Vengeance."

"We can still stop this!" Jaccob said. "Turn me on. Power me up! *Computer!*"

Antonio shook his head. "I cannot let you interfere. You—"

"This is my family!" Jaccob shouted. "You have to let me go! Please!"

Antonio hesitated, distracted, and that was just enough for Jaccob to launch a desperate left hook. Blind on that side, Antonio couldn't have seen it coming. He rocked back. As the pressure loosened, Jaccob wrestled his way free. He fell off the SUV and ran toward a pair of shoppers who were coming down to find their car.

"Protectorate business!" he shouted by reflex, hand raised. "I need your—"

"Aah!" They both screamed and ran away from the wild-eyed man in the shiny blue power suit pointing a repulsor at them. The woman threw down her purse and the man tossed him a set of keys.

"—Keys," Jaccob said, then clicked the beeper to locate their car. A red Corvette. Perfect.

He passed the Raven on the way out of the parking lot, but the man only looked at him with his one-eyed glare. He gave Jaccob a slight nod.

Jaccob gunned it and sped toward his family.

CHAPTER TWELVE

SCRAPPERS

Lady Vengeance was already moving when the shotgun went off, and she managed to deflect the blast with the fearsword. She felt the shell shear through some of her gathered power, even as the force lifted her off her feet and sent her on a shattering journey backward through the just-repaired bay window into the kitchen.

It took her a moment to decide which way was up. Her head was aching from the thunderous report of the shotgun as much as the creeping hangover. Up until an hour ago, she thought she'd still been drunk, but now she felt painfully sober. And, of course, she was undeniably in serious shit.

"She survives." Havana climbed in through the broken window. She'd paused to slip into some sandals—no sense cutting her feet on all the broken glass.

Magdalena stalked through the sliding glass doors, shotgun raised. "Good."

"Caution," Havana said. "We have orders to take her alive, sister."

"Huginn and Muninn," Lady Vengeance said. "I see you still have that creepy, pseudo-incestuous mythology thing going."

Magdalena glared at her. "Alive but critically wounded is alive, sister."

"*Verdad.*" Havana raised her katana, which glinted in the afternoon light.

Lady Vengeance struggled to her feet, fearsword held in a low, defensive stance. The two women weren't quite flanking her, but they purposefully stayed far enough apart she had to look back and forth between them. Magdalena's shotgun presented the chief threat, but she couldn't underestimate Havana's speed. Worse, she saw Mike peeking at her from around the wall by the kitchen, Chuck was tugging at his arm. Lady Vengeance tried to shake her head subtly, but the Raven twins clearly noticed.

"*No preocupes*," said Magdalena. "I'll deal with the witnesses."

"Just fucking *go*!" Lady Vengeance shouted at Mike, her voice tainted with her demonic manifestation. "Take care of your sister!"

Eyes wide, the kids scampered off.

"Surprising," Havana said. "She cares about the children."

"Tactical collateral," Magdalena said. "I'll collect them."

"Over my fabulous corpse, maybe," Lady Vengeance said, raising her sword.

The Raven twins exchanged a look. "*Bueno*," Havana said, even as Magdalena said, "Fine."

Lady Vengeance went straight for Magdalena, blade high, hoping to surprise her. No such luck: a shotgun blast sent her flying back, right at Havana. Lady Vengeance landed, clashing swords before she even had her footing. They danced around each other on top of the counter, amongst the broken glass. Lady Vengeance was glad she'd turned down the cute heels at Nordstrom. Lady Vengeance could only parry about three of Havana's cuts before she had to swing back toward Magdalena to deflect a shotgun blast. It winged her, and she toppled through some hanging pots and pans and off the counter. The fearsword fell out of her hand and shattered to nothing on the floor. She landed on her stomach, her hands twitching as they searched the floor around her.

"*Simple*." Havana sounded almost disappointed as she raised her sword up.

Lady Vengeance rolled over, slapped the katana aside with her claw, then slammed the frying pan in her other hand as hard as she could into Havana's knee. The woman cried out in pain and surprise, and Lady Vengeance seized the chance to swing the pan at her head. Havana blocked it with her left arm, which made a creaking sound against the metal bludgeon. She staggered away against the opposite wall.

"Who needs a fearsword?" Lady Vengeance hefted the frying pan. "Now they're going to start calling me the *Panhandler*."

Then Magdalena came around the counter, clearing a shot, and Lady Vengeance realized a frying pan wasn't going to stop it. She needed another second to re-summon her fearsword—a second she wasn't going to get.

A high-pitched whine filled the air, and a blast of force lifted Magdalena off her feet and hurled her out the window and into the pool. A second later, her shotgun splashed into the water with a disconsolate *plunk*.

Mike stepped into the kitchen, an old-model Starband gauntlet on his arm. "I know where Dad keeps the big guns!" he shouted.

Chuck was there too, standing just to the side of her brother. A shimmering blue aura surrounded her, projected from her wristwatch. It was a personal forcefield similar to the one generated by the Stardust armor. Lady Vengeance wished she had one of those.

"Thanks, kids," Lady Vengeance said. "Now get out!"

"I can help!" Mike pointed the repulsor at Havana, but instead of a blast it just let out a depressed whine and a plume of smoke. "Piece of crap."

Havana stepped toward Mike, but Lady Vengeance jumped on her and swatted the katana aside with the frying pan. Mike's renewed fear filled her, and she conjured her fearsword again in time to catch Havana's counter. "Go!"

A drenched Magdalena leaped back in, hands filled with two blazing handguns. Lady Vengeance didn't have time to dwell on wondering where she'd kept those in her bikini. Some of the bullets strayed toward Chuck, but they bounced off her shimmering blue forcefield. The girl was the sensible one, going defensive. She took after her mother, which in this case was a serious plus.

"Chuck, grab your idiot brother and get out of here!" Lady Vengeance shouted.

This time, the kids ran off and didn't come back.

Lady Vengeance fought both Ravenettes at once, weaving first to deflect a string of Magdalena's bullets with her fearsword, then back to parry Havana's katana aside with the much-nicked frying pan. She turned constantly to focus on one of the twins while she channeled fear energy to guard against the other. After so long without a proper fight, she lost her breath quickly, but she couldn't deny the thrill of battle.

"She is tiring," Havana said.

Magdalena agreed. "She will lose."

"You think so?" Lady Vengeance clenched her teeth. "The old Raven taught Tony and me to fight before either of you graduated to sippy cups. Also ... you're afraid."

It was true. Lady Vengeance might be older and overmatched, but the longer the fight lasted, the more uneasy the twins became. Lady Vengeance absorbed their growing fear, which flowed into her skin, changing it. This was the third way in which her powers worked: given the chance and a particularly specific fear, she could become the object of that fear. It was potentially the most powerful use of her talent, but also the least predictable. She'd done well lasting this long, but they'd wear her down eventually. She had to take the chance.

Her fearsword and armor dimmed as Lady Vengeance redirected the fear she had taken from Liz, the kids, and the twins. Her skin darkened, her clothes shifted into a suit of black metal, and one of her eyes lit with red light.

Lady Vengeance had become the Raven.

"He is your fear, eh?" she asked in his voice. "You fear your master. *Kinky.*"

Unfortunately, it wasn't direct confrontation they feared, and they kept fighting just as fiercely as before. And without her fearsword, Lady Vengeance could not defeat them. She blocked one last katana slash and faced two pistols with no way to stop them. She sucked in a breath, but the bullets didn't come. The guns clicked empty.

"Well, that was lucky," she said.

Then Magdalena pistol-whipped her in the face and she fell to her knees, blood trickling down her chin. Such delicious blood.

Hear me, the voice said, and she did.

The twins circled around her, their faces filled with anger.

"How dare she take his face," Havana put her sword to Lady Vengeance's throat. "I will kill her."

"Let me." Magdalena was loading fresh clips into her pistols. "The bitch dies."

"The bitch is right here," Lady Vengeance said with a smile. "Girls, I was born that way, and I'll die that way. Stop talking about it and just do it."

The twins looked confused, particularly so when Lady Vengeance started laughing. At first, they were just giggles, but they quickly grew to loud, insane laughter.

"You think you've won? Do you?" She spoke in a voice neither hers nor the Raven's—a voice that matched her jet-black eyes. "She's not alone in here, you know."

~

"Come on, come on!" Jaccob said as he streaked toward the cabin. "Go faster!"

He drove his stolen car—stolen!—through the winding roads toward the cabin. Invoking the old team had been a reflex, and now it filled him with bittersweet nostalgia and anxiety. If any of them were still in the game, he could have had Kara Sparx and Lumien babysit the kids and not worry about it. Well, worry a little, but only based on the substantial property damage from the shenanigans that would definitely ensue.

Now he was the last of the Protectorate still active, and he had only a crazy alcoholic empath (who may or may not be possessed) to rely upon. Things looked dire.

"C'mon, c'mon!"

Having grown up on video games and carried the hobby into adulthood, he knew how to drive, but 90 mph was as fast as he could push the Corvette without ending up in a tree. His mind flew faster than that, whipping through a million possibilities.

"The cabin could be in flames," Jaccob said. "My family might be horribly murdered. A meteor could be hurtling toward the earth, trailing frogs. I might have to get up before eight on a Saturday. All sorts of perversions of natural law."

The ridiculousness kept down the panic that bottled up in his chest. He couldn't even call Liz, without his armor's communication systems active.

"Jaccob, we need to talk," said the Computer.

"I'm not speaking to you right now," Jaccob said. "Well, literally I am, but—damn it, Computer, how could you?"

"It is not entirely my fault, Jaccob," said the Computer. "I am working to purge my server of his influence. But until I do—"

"Yeah, yeah, you need time to get over him, blah blah blah," Jaccob said. "Can you at least patch me through to him?"

There was a pause. "Stand by."

Two seconds later, the Raven's voice sounded in Jaccob's ear. "It's too late, Jaccob Stevens," he said. "Your damsel in distress will do anything to win, which is a commendable quality in anyone but her. I have seen the havoc she will wreak when—"

"I swear to you," Jaccob said, "that if my wife or my kids are hurt, I will make you pay. That's a promise."

That seemed to surprise the Raven. "If they do not interfere, they will not be hurt," he said at length. "Understand. Stopping that monster is more important."

Jaccob bit his tongue to keep from screaming. "Have you tried, I don't know, *helping* her, rather than hurting her? Tried to see her as a human being, maybe?"

The Raven responded with an even longer silence. "More than you know."

The connection cut off.

"What does that mean?" Jaccob asked. "Is 'being cryptic' one of his powers?"

Not that he had time to think about it or overly cared just then.

Abruptly, his power cells whirred into life, and his armor came back on.

"Full power," said the Computer. "Antonio Desantes is gone from my local server. He still owns Admin rights at the Tower, but I am uncompromised in the armor."

"Uncompromised?" Was it a coincidence, or by design? Had he said something that made the Raven reconsider? Regardless ... "All right!" Jaccob shouted.

He switched on his boot-jets and shot into the air. Behind him, the now-driverless and on-fire Corvette exploded off the road and into the forest.

"Should have noted the license plate number," Stardust murmured. "Oh well."

He soared toward the cabin, praying he'd make it in time.

~

"She's not alone in here, you know."

With all her energy wasted, she wasn't a hero anymore—not Lady Vengeance anymore. She was barely Vivienne Cain anymore. She felt worn out, defeated. Azazel's laughter echoed in her ears, and his voice was close to her lips. She had just a scrap of will left, and it was faltering ...

"She really isn't," said an entirely new voice, behind them.

Havana hissed a warning and Magdalena raised her guns. A *second* Lady Vengeance had joined them in the kitchen, this one fresh and burning with power. She held a bright fearsword in her hands, and she wore black and purple armor identical to what Vivienne had worn when she entered the cabin.

"No," Vivienne said, but no one was listening.

"What is this, sister?" asked Havana.

Magdalena raised her pistols, one at each Lady Vengeance.

"That's quite enough, Mrs. Stevens," the newcomer said. "Your kids are safe."

What are you doing? Vivienne wanted to shout but talking now would get them both killed.

"*No comprendo,*" said Havana, and Magdalena nodded.

"*Comprendo* this, girls: you're attacking the wrong woman," Liz said in Vivienne's voice, through the illusion of Lady Vengeance. "Liz left me in the car while she rushed in to protect her kids, disguised with some gizmo. Here."

They looked confused, until Liz slowly drew a small controller from her pocket and tossed it toward Vivienne. She caught it, and it must have been preset, because instantly Vivienne became Liz. They faced the twins in the blown-up kitchen, both women looking like the other. Clearly one of them was the woman they'd come to capture, and the other someone they absolutely shouldn't take.

Don't do this, Vivienne wanted to say, but she held her silence.

"This is a trick," Magdalena said, fingers tightening on the triggers.

Liz as Vivienne scoffed. "You really think I care about those little turds? Good riddance. But Liz—she's their mom. Me, I finally got bored with the whole stupid thing and figured I'd put a stop to it. I'd rather be captured than have to put up with one more minute of her whiny, entitled crap." She put out her hands to be handcuffed.

The twins shared a look. "We'll take them both," Magdalena said.

Havana shook her head. "And have Stardust rushing out to save his wife?"

The sound of sirens filtered into the room, and Vivienne's heart picked up faster. *Good job, Chuck*, she thought. Calling for the cavalry when the time was right.

Vivienne could feel fear growing in the twins, and she realized finally what they truly feared—and why she had become their master. It wasn't confrontation they dreaded, but failure. They could not go back to the Raven without Lady Vengeance in custody. But if they took Stardust's wife, the Raven would be furious.

The twins had to make a decision, and fast. At length, they nodded to each other.

Havana drew her sword. "*Lo siento, señora.*"

PART FOUR

THIS TIME, IT'S PERSONAL

CHAPTER THIRTEEN

STARDUST UNLEASHED

Half a dozen police cars were clustered outside the cabin when Stardust swooped down onto the porch. His appearance startled the cops, but he strode right past them without a word. The cabin was an absolute mess: the kitchen destroyed and gaping out into the backyard. A number of cops dusted for prints around the pool.

"Where's my family?" Stardust asked the nearest cop.

Startled at his thick voice, the red-haired woman replied with a stutter and wide eyes. She pointed to the living room, where Mike and Chuck sat on either side of Liz. The kids' faces lit up when they saw their father, but they looked too dazed to do more than look. Liz immediately looked away, her expression apologetic.

"Leave," Stardust said quietly. "Now."

Some of the cops looked over at him, but most of the conversations kept on. "Sir," said the red-haired cop. "We have to—"

"Take it up with the chief," Stardust said to her without looking. He turned on Stardust's speakers, and energy crackled around his Starbands. "Get out. *Now!*"

That drew everyone's attention to a Stardust they didn't often see. Jaccob kept his eyes fixed on his family as the cops filed out of the room.

"Where is she?" Jaccob asked when they were gone.

Liz's bright eyes gleamed at him. "Mike, Chuck, give us a minute?"

The kids looked confused, but they did as she said. They went downstairs to the screening room, and within seconds, loud music started up.

"Where is she?" Jaccob's voice deepened as anger rose in him.

She shook her head. "They took her. The Raven's henchwomen."

Something broke inside Jaccob, and he could hardly keep hold of his breath. His Starbands crackled. "Are you all right, Jaccob?" asked the Computer.

"I'll ask one more time," Jaccob said. "Where is she?" He glared, and full power flowed into his armor. "Where is my *wife*?"

The image of Liz wavered and failed, turning into Lady Vengeance, who set the image inducer on the couch next to her. She sighed. "Look, I—"

He hit her with a flying tackle, shot out the back wall, and up into the night.

~

Carried aloft in Stardust's arms at a rapid pace, Vivienne coughed and sputtered and strained to keep her head from exploding at the rapid pressure change. As it was, pain like the worst migraine she'd ever had ripped through her head.

"Much," she mumbled. "Much ... would have preferred ... Bora Bora."

For his part, Stardust seemed to care absolutely nothing for how hard the trip would be on his unwilling passenger. He carried her up and up, as implacable and unstoppable as a space shuttle. They flew level with a passing jetliner, and up and up. Did Stardust mean to fly her into outer space?

Finally, he paused and stared at her, hovering at 30,000 feet, give or take. He seemed fine in his armor, while she gasped for breath that just would not come. Also, her body didn't seem capable of anything but shivering. She'd only halfway paid attention to Antonio's stories about climbing Everest, but she remembered his vivid description of living at that altitude. How once you hit a certain altitude, your body just started dying. And she had neither a coat nor supplemental oxygen to stave it off.

Tony, she thought. *Should've let Tony shoot me in the head. Better than freezing and/or wheezing to death.*

Storm clouds swirled around them, and all was dark and cold.

"My family?" Stardust demanded, his speakers thundering in her ears. "You brought my *family* into this? You got my wife captured? You *coward*!"

"Nnh."

Suddenly she was not alone, however. She hadn't had a thing to drink for hours—Liz Stevens, after all, didn't drink, and Vivienne had done a pretty good job passing as her. And now, as sobriety loomed, so too did the darkness inside.

Let go, Azazel said in her mind. *Let me in.*

Vivienne pushed it aside. If she was going to die, at least she could die as herself.

"Was this your plan all along?" Stardust screamed at her. "Or the demon's?"

Vivienne was choking, her eyes filling with what looked and felt like watery pus. Her body grew tight, closing in on itself. Was this what death felt like? A horrible death.

The death she deserved.

"Dammit." Stardust did something, and his forcefield expanded to surround them both. Air vented out of his armor, filling her lungs so suddenly she almost passed out. She coughed and vomited on his blue suit.

His crackling gauntlet closed around her throat—not tight enough to choke her, but enough that she felt it. That, and his overpowering anger and terror. Jaccob Stevens had never been so scared in all his life.

"You thought you could get away with this?" Stardust asked. "Was this your plan all along? What, you trick your way into my house and what, replace my wife?"

"Oh yes," Vivienne said. "Ooh, Jaccob Stevens, gotta get me some of *that*."

Spit in the devil's eye. Vivienne had never been good at submission.

Stardust's visor mostly hid his face, but he did *not* look amused. "My wife gave you everything. I wanted to throw you in prison, but no, she argued me down. She fed you. She sheltered you. And for what? You betrayed her and fed her to those *monsters*."

Vivienne coughed and shook her head as much as she could. "H and M aren't so bad," she said. "Once you get past the psychotic bitch thing."

Stardust actually *growled* at her. "You have to be a demon," he said. "You *have* to be! No human being would have—"

"Shit happens, Shiny," Vivienne said. "Maybe you don't see it, from your shiny tower of awesomeness. But *shit. Happens.*"

"You did this," Stardust said. "You. If you hadn't come into our lives—*God*!"

His fear suffused her, providing so much power she felt drunk. It was enough to defeat a thousand Stardusts in a thousand worlds.

I can save you, Azazel whispered. *Let me in. Together, we will—*

Vivienne pushed the demon deeper down and focused on Jaccob. "It wasn't my choice, all right?" she said. "I fought both of the Raven's little bitches to save your little brats—the one that idolizes me and the one that beats off to me—and for what? So your stupid wife could throw herself to the wolves. Yeah, that's right." She sneered in reply to Stardust's surprised expression. "She used the image bullshit-thingy to look like me, and then convinced the Raven sluts to take her instead."

"She did that?" Stardust was catching on. "She—"

"I know, right?" Vivienne said. "None of them were supposed to get hurt, and her children were already safe. I don't know why she was so stupid."

"Because she's a good person, Vengeance," Stardust said. "Because she can't stand to see someone suffer."

Vivienne shook her head. "She was still an idiot."

"*You!*" Stardust seethed. "You brought this down upon us. I wish I'd never met you. You ruined my *life*!"

The darkness surged up in her, and she could not say if the demon said it or she did. "Ha!" Vivienne smiled crazily, her head lolling. "Don't tell me you're not pleased."

"Pleased?" The half of Stardust's face she could see beneath his visor turned grey and his voice softened. "What do you mean?"

"With your newfound freedom, Stardust," Vivienne said. "No wife, kids remanded to CPS. Just this. It's what you want, isn't it?" She put her hand up to his visor as though to caress his face. "There's no point in denying it. I'm an empath, remember?" She pressed a little closer to him. "I know you want this, even if you can't admit it."

"But—" Stardust shivered under her touch. "But I—"

"That's right," Vivienne said. "You may act all good and noble, but underneath, you're just like Antonio and me. This isn't your life—not the one you're meant to have."

He trembled but said nothing as she leaned up to his half-covered face.

"You aren't Jaccob Stevens." Vivienne lifted his visor. "You're Stardust."

She kissed him.

~

As Stardust hovered there, kissing Lady Vengeance, it all crashed in on him. His kids felt increasingly distant: he'd embarrassed Chuck on their shopping trip, then embarrassed Mike at the cabin. He argued so much with Liz, who always seemed to nag him. His work no longer encouraged or excited him. It was only when he put on the armor of Stardust—when he jetted around fighting villainy and rescuing Cobalt City—that he felt anything like excitement or fulfillment. What if ...

What if she was *right*?

"You know I'm right." Lady Vengeance's eyes glowed jet-black. "You know I am."

"But—" Stardust trembled.

"Come with me," she said. "Come with me, and—"

"Oh my God, you—" Stardust thrust her away, so abruptly and hard he almost dropped her. He held her outside the forcefield again, and she choked on the freezing air again. "I see it now. The Raven was right: you're a *monster*."

"Heh, join the club." Starting to shiver, Lady Vengeance looked around at the spiraling clouds around them. "Well, what are you waiting for? Drop me already."

Stardust stared. "You—you want to die, is that it? You want me to kill you?"

"Sure, why not?" Lady Vengeance smiled. "At this point, you can't honestly think I don't deserve it. After what I've done? How many people I've hurt? You have no idea."

"That's why you were in Valhalla," Stardust said. "You wanted him to kill you. And now, since he didn't do it, you're trying to get me to do the job. Right?"

"I just—I just want it to be over," she said. "I—"

"Why, Vivienne Cain?" he roared. "Why didn't you just let him kill you? Why do I have to be the one that does it?"

"Because—" She coughed. "Because you're ... you're a better man. You—"

Lady Vengeance tried to say more but could only cough up dark liquid. Blood seeped down her shirt as well. The stress on her body had broken open the old wound, and there were no nanobots to repair her this time. If she wanted to die, the altitude would grant that soon.

Stardust found absolutely no desire to pull her back into the safety of the forcefield. He had never hated anyone as much as he hated her, right then and there. A different part of him spoke—one he had never thought existed—a part of him that *wanted* her to die.

Kill her, said a voice he did not know. *Let us be what you were meant to be.*

Something broke inside Stardust, and he knew exactly what to do.

He drew the ailing Lady Vengeance back into the forcefield. She looked up at him, confused. "You're not ... you're not going to kill me?"

"If you could save Liz," he said, "you would, wouldn't you?"

Lady Vengeance stared at him a long time before she nodded slowly.

"Then you aren't a monster," he said. "Liz was right. If you were half the villain the Raven thinks you are, you wouldn't be punishing yourself like this. You wouldn't hate yourself as much as you do. You might have your horrible moments, but you aren't a villain and you aren't controlled by a demon. You're just a psychotic, suicidal bitch."

"Ha, don't ... spare my feelings ... or anything."

"You didn't kill all your friends, did you?" Stardust asked.

"Liz doesn't think so," Lady Vengeance says.

"She *is* a good judge of character," Stardust said. "So if you're innocent, why does he hate you so much—the Raven?"

"Does it really matter?" Lady Vengeance asked.

"Not especially." Stardust shrugged.

Lady Vengeance coughed. "Well, if you aren't going to drop me, can we go back to the ground now? I need a drink in the worst way."

Stardust wrapped his arms awkwardly around her and started the descent.

As they were flying down—a much more pleasant trip when both were inside the forcefield—Lady Vengeance cleared her throat. "I'm sorry, by the way—about the thing."

"What thing?"

Lady Vengeance looked awkward. "The kissing thing."

Stardust coughed. "Oh, that thing."

"I was just playing on your fear. It's very strong." She closed her eyes. "It sometimes takes a few tries to figure out someone's biggest fear, but not with you. I got it the first time, and every time since: you're afraid of losing them. If you at all doubt that you love your wife and kids, don't."

"No, I know." He nodded. "Let's go kick the crap out of a bad guy."

Lady Vengeance smiled. "He'll power drain me at first sight. You got a sword I can borrow?"

"I'll do you one better." Stardust nodded. "We can borrow Chuck's forcefield watch. You still have that image inducer?"

"Down at the cabin. Why?"

Stardust looked excited. "I have an idea."

"That's what I like to hear." She bit her lip. "You know he won't stop. He won't give up. There's only one thing that will make this end."

"I know," he said. "One of you has to die."

~

The sun would not rise for an hour yet, but light had just started creeping over the horizon. The view from the penthouse atop Starcom Tower was really quite spectacular, almost like the Raven's own Colorado mountain sanctuary in Valhalla. In his lap, he held the deactivated image inducer, which he found legitimately fascinating. It represented a kind of tech he'd never even considered, with wires and gizmos like something out of a pulp sci-fi novel or a steampunk movie. He couldn't create something like this and doubted he would have much luck reverse engineering it either. In his vision of how things were supposed to work, this made no sense.

"This isn't going to work, you know," said Liz Stevens, where she sat cuffed at the other end of the dinner table. Two glasses of wine—untouched—stood before her. "My husband will come rescue me. Absolutely."

The Raven looked away. "I expect Lady Vengeance will defeat him—or perhaps he'll kill her, and my task will be done. Regardless, I won't be fighting him."

"Unless she seduces him and they run off together. Ever thought of that?"

The Raven shrugged. "You saw them in the forest, and yet you said nothing."

"Is this where you try to drive a wedge between us?" Liz asked. "C'mon. Do the villain thing. Empathize with our marital problems."

"I suspect that would be wasted effort," the Raven said. "And I would rather not step between a husband and wife." Then, softer: "Not again."

"Huh." Liz nodded. "If you know he'll come, why hold me? Why risk it?"

"Because it sets him off balance," the Raven said. "If you are in danger, he will make mistakes. He will not attack if he thinks you are at risk."

"So you're holding me captive *because* he loves me."

"*Verdad.*"

The Raven rose and crossed to the balcony railing, where he could see all of Cobalt City laid out below him. He knew all too well the foolishness of a man in love.

"Why bother to cuff me at all?" Liz asked. "If you've hacked into all the security systems and control the building, it's not like I'm going anywhere."

"It would be the height of arrogance to underestimate such a capable woman in her own house." The Raven returned from the railing and sat on the edge of the table near her. He positioned himself in such a way that she could only see his left profile. "I am impressed; you don't seem the least bit afraid."

"Confident," she said. "My husband steamrolls petty villains like you all the time."

"I am a villain, then?"

"You don't think so? All the damage Vivienne has done so far has been in response to your attacks. The way I see it, the one who causes the terror is the terrorist."

The Raven smiled. "By all means, try to win my sympathies with flattery."

"No need." Liz shook her head. "You wouldn't hurt me, even if you wanted to. You're not stupid enough to make Jaccob your enemy. You lay a finger on me, and he won't stop until you're dead."

"You call him Jaccob." The Raven lifted one of the unclaimed wine glasses to his lips. "As though that makes him a man, rather than a thing."

"Like you—*Raven.*"

He didn't seem troubled by the logic. "Regardless, Stardust is not a killer."

"I don't think you are either," Liz said. "The way Jaccob described your attack on the police station—you could have killed any of those officers, and yet you went out of your way to prevent any casualties. You sent your girls to my house with standing orders not to hurt anyone but Vivienne. You're a good man, even if you're better at hiding it."

The Raven looked at her fully now, and the light glinted strangely on his right eye, which was glass. "*¿Verdad?*"

"Yes." She smiled. "Under different circumstances, we might have been friends."

The Raven looked away. "You mean circumstances in which I didn't blow up your house, threaten your children, and lure your husband into a trap."

"Pretty much." Liz bit her lip. "Why do you hate her so much? I mean, I know all about Supergroup, about your battle, all of it. I know she didn't do it, and if I worked that out in just a couple days, you must not still believe she's guilty. You're trying to punish her for something she didn't even do? This isn't justice."

There was a long pause, in which the Raven slowly drained his wine.

Finally, the Raven shook his head. "It does not matter. It never did. She is the death of this world, and if I am the only one who will see that, then so be it."

Liz sighed. "She misses you, you know," she said. "I don't know what happened between you, but I know that."

The Raven opened his mouth to respond, but an alert beeped on the proximity scanners. A positive ID on Vivienne Cain. He sighed.

"Good chat." The Raven picked up a prepared syringe. "I'm going to have to put you under now."

Liz tensed, her fingers digging into the arms of her chair. "Do what you have to," she said. "Only—don't hurt anyone you don't have to, all right?"

"Yes." The Raven nodded. "You should have some of the wine. It makes the drugs gentler."

Liz nodded. She reached for her wine, but the cuffs stopped her hands short. The Raven picked up her glass and tipped it to her lips.

"I hope your husband does the right thing," he said.

CHAPTER FOURTEEN

INFILTRATION

"Well, here we go," Lady Vengeance said as she strode into the Starcom lobby. She wore black leather, a long trenchcoat, her silver claw strapped to her left hand, and a katana sheathed at her belt. Also sunglasses, because Stardust had insisted.

The reaction was instantaneous. Wild-eyed receptionists called for police and security, then retreated into panic rooms. Red lights flashed as heavily armed soldiers poured out of side doors. Sirens whined as police rushed to the scene. Guns cocked all around her as men shouted at her to drop the claws and put her hands on her head.

Lady Vengeance looked at all the men, with their delicious fears she'd been absorbing since she got off the bus within a hundred yards of Starcom Tower. All that fear energy had built and built in her, but she hadn't yet shaped it.

She smiled.

Black flames swirled around her, billowing forth in a whirlwind that filled the chamber. Lightning flashed, the air cracked open, and a hulking *thing* strode forth. It stood on cloven hooves, a creature half-man/half-bear, and glared at the Starcom Security Corps with glowing purple eyes. It raised up a jagged sword that looked like a rusted meat cleaver.

"I am Azazel, Prince of Hell," Lady Vengeance said, her deep voice loud and resonant. "I own this body, as I will own your souls!"

Some of the guards shuddered and fell back, some turned and fled, and some opened fire. The demon roared and strode forward to attack, sweeping the black fire along with it like wings. Bullets sprayed, and the cries of men filled the room.

Meanwhile, Lady Vengeance slipped through the confusion and into the private executive elevator. Inside, she scanned Stardust's security badge and hit the button for the penthouse. As the numbers counted upward at an increasingly rapid pace, she drew her katana. Conjuring the illusory demon with the image inducer and powering it with fear energy to occupy security had drained most of the fear she'd absorbed, but she had the sword and plenty of training.

Around floor 30, Lady Vengeance scratched at her backside. Her creaking new black leathers—purchased during her shopping trip at the mall—didn't fit as well as her old outfit had. Alas, after a week of fighting, it was damaged beyond repair. Oh well.

"Tights *are* so overrated," she murmured.

There was a presence in the elevator with her, but it only served to make her smile. The Raven may have taken over the tower itself, but Starcom Tower's spirit would not be so easy to enslave. How amusing, that for all his technological know-how, Stardust himself never seemed to understand what she was talking about when she mentioned the Spirit, but to her—attuned to emotion as she was, and a spirit was mostly emotion—it seemed so clear. The spirit urged her to free its dear friend Computer.

"I will," Lady Vengeance whispered. "One way or another."

The elevator dinged at the penthouse level, and Lady Vengeance braced for an arcing sword or a hail of bullets. Neither came, however, and she stood tense against the wall of the elevator for several pulse-pounding seconds before she finally slipped through the doors.

The Stevens family penthouse was sumptuous, modern, and comfortable. Clearly, Liz had done most of the decorating, from the impressionist and cubist paintings to the many hanging vines. No doubt, Jaccob would have filled the penthouse with posters from 70s or 80s metal bands or worse—*90s* metal bands. Lady Vengeance cleared each room, katana high and ready, but no ambush waited. She made her way slowly to the dining room, lit by cool, pre-dawn light. The first rays of the morning dazzled her, and she squinted to make out the dark shapes at the table.

One was Liz Stevens, unmoving and apparently dazed. With her empathy, Lady Vengeance sensed that she was alive but drugged or otherwise incapacitated. At the other end of the table, Antonio Desantes sat staring off into the sunrise. Lady Vengeance could feel his emotions from the hallway: contentment, mostly, tinged with that constant paranoid anxiety that was the hallmark of the Raven. There was no anger or fear there, and she almost convinced herself that she'd managed to sneak up on him. Then he reached out and almost casually pressed a button on a controller in his hand.

The walls around her lit with a green light, and Lady Vengeance realized what was happening only an instant before the pain began. He'd brought a power dampener.

Her connection to Antonio's emotions vanished in a wave of overwhelming pain. It felt like the device seized her from all different angles and pulled with the strength of a dozen super-bruisers. Her insides turned into her outsides and her head exploded with a heavy bass drum kick, over and over until she fell to her knees, moaning.

Antonio didn't seem the least bit troubled. "I remember sunrises like this," he said without looking at her. "We used to stay up and watch them together."

She gritted her teeth. "Don't ... go all ... sentimental, Tony."

"You call me by my human name, as though that will delay what we both know I must do." Antonio put the remote back on the table and stood to face her. "I expected you'd come, but I am also disappointed you were so easy to trap."

"You know me—easy." She could almost move without wave upon wave of nausea. If she kept him talking just another minute, maybe she could lift her sword. "Dick move with the dampener. But then, you always were afraid to face me like a man."

"I only want to contain your demon," said the Raven. "You alone do not frighten me. But when you give in and hand the demon your powers ... I am a cautious man."

"A chicken-shit *bitch* is more like it."

"I am doing what must be done."

He waved—a pre-determined signal—and his two Ravenettes stalked into the kitchen. Magdalena kept Lady Vengeance covered with an assault rifle while Havana took the katana from her limp hand. The two had lost the bikinis and instead wore the sleek power suits he'd fashioned for them. How the Raven doted on his girls—spies, assassins, lovers, etc. At least they weren't *actually* sisters.

"Never made one of those ... for me, Tony," Lady Vengeance said. "I'm jealous."

The Raven brushed off the comment and waved to the twins to search her. They unstrapped her claw and set it on the table, as well as her image inducer, which the Raven shut off. At just that moment, Azazel downstairs would be disappearing.

"Wait," Magdalena said. "What's that?"

She pointed to Lady Vengeance's wrist, where she wore a familiar watch—Chuck's watch. Of course they'd remember the forcefield from the fight at the cabin. The girls relieved her of that too, and the Raven set it on the table. The Raven ignored the watch and inspected the image inducer a moment—perhaps comparing it to the one Liz had used. Finally, he shook his head and turned back to Lady Vengeance. "I half expected Stardust would dispose of you. There would be no need for battle then."

"There's no need for your hostage now." Lady Vengeance nodded at Liz. "Let her go. She has no part in this."

"Not until you are dead," the Raven said. "We do not need Stardust interfering."

Lady Vengeance had expected he might say something like that, which was why she'd made plan B. With the Raven fixated on her and distracted, Lady Vengeance saw the image inducer whir quietly to life. This function hadn't been tested yet, so she had to keep the Raven distracted while it started up, then hope it worked.

"You've always been a bad sport, Tony," Lady Vengeance said. "Three against one? Not to mention all those security guards you sent against me? Not really your style. Getting lazy in your middle age?"

Magdalena's face turned red. She'd always been the emotional one. "She insults you, Master. Let me kill her, *por favor*."

"*Cállate*." The Raven glared at her, and Magdalena suddenly found her feet very, very interesting. "I will kill her. No one else."

"Keeping their hands clean, huh? How sweet," Lady Vengeance said. "After all, our hands are already pretty dirty. No risk there."

"You should be silent and die with honor." The Raven held out his hand, and Havana gave him the katana, which he tested through the air twice. He nodded.

Come on, she thought to the image inducer. *Boot up*.

The Raven put the sword to her throat. Lady Vengeance was out of time.

"This is what awaits you, Ravenettes," she said. "Either you become him—a bitter, scarred murderer—or else he kills you and laughs doing it. Don't forget."

Appealing to H and M would do no good, of course, but it got the Raven's attention. He looked at her with something Lady Vengeance thought might be sadness. "Your death gives me no pleasure, Vivienne Cain. Only—"

"Bullshit," Lady Vengeance said. "We all know what a great liar you are—hell, even *I* believed you twenty years ago. You know, when you told me you didn't love me."

That gave them all pause. The Raven sisters looked startled—whatever they had heard about Lady Vengeance, they must not have expected something like *that*. The Raven himself hesitated.

And that was just long enough for the light on the image inducer to turn green. Immediately, it projected a ray of light—not toward Lady Vengeance and the man about to execute her, but toward Liz Stevens. It surrounded her in a bubble of wavering blue light. A forcefield. They also heard the muted intro of an upbeat rock song.

"*¿Qué es esto?*" Magdalena asked.

Havana pointed to the forcefield. "*¡Maestro, mira!*"

The Raven glanced over, then back to Lady Vengeance. "Why protect her, and not yourself?"

"I try to avoid collateral damage when I beat the snot out of someone."

"Did you honestly think you could face us by yourself?" the Raven asked.

Lady Vengeance scoffed. "Tsch, no."

The rock music wasn't coming from the emitter, but rather seemingly from the walls themselves. It grew louder, and they heard the sound of boot-jets humming.

"You didn't think I'd come alone, did you?" Lady Vengeance asked.

Then the ceiling shattered in a swell of rock and the *z-zap!* of Starbolts. Stardust blasted through into the kitchen, sending dust and concrete flying in every direction. He crashed down between Lady Vengeance and the Raven, speakers blaring.

"Great theme music, right?" he shouted.

Then he punched the Raven in the chest, which put him through the wall into the living room.

Stardust probably would have followed, but H and M jumped him from both sides. He sent one flying with a Starbolt and turned to fend off the other.

Lady Vengeance reclaimed her sword and got to her feet. She stepped around them, grabbed her claw and the wristwatch from the table, and made a beeline toward where Antonio was climbing off a knocked-over couch. "I am so going to kick your ass."

The Raven shook his head to clear it, and his power suit unfolded from beneath his coat, which itself grew into his cloak of razor feathers. One red eye burned in the face of his raptor helmet. He caught her first cut on his spiked gauntlet. He shoved her back and extended a long blade from his right gauntlet—almost like a sword of his own.

"Nevermore, mother fucker," she said.

"*Bueno*," he said.

~

Stardust had to confess, it was a good plan. Protecting Liz was his top priority, so he'd modified Lady Vengeance's image inducer to project the same forcefield he used in his armor. And she had managed to get it within the five feet it needed to work, basically walking into a personal death trap. Stardust was amazed: that woman had guts.

Not that going all comet-action on his tower penthouse and landing perfectly between them all was easy. But hey, he could be modest—if he tried really hard.

One of the twins—Magdalena, Lady Vengeance had called her, which reminded him of a song from somewhere—was circling, riddling his forcefield with bullets. He'd changed the frequency of his field from "opposition" to "inertial dampener," which made the bullets just stop when they touched the field, then gently drift to the ground when he moved away. It also looked insanely cool. He could safely ignore Magdalena and focus instead on Havana, who danced around him, looking for an opening to put her sword.

"Sorry, kid," he said. "The Stardust forcefield 2.0 is just impenetrable. There's no way a flimsy little sword—"

She hit a button on the hilt, and the blade started vibrating with enough speed to give off a high-pitched whine. A vibroblade. Great.

Not only that, but she leaped up, gouged a long slit in the ceiling, and a satellite dish crashed down above him. His field tried to stop the dish—he could almost feel the effort—but it was simply too big. It crushed him beneath it, driving him into the floor.

"Now what?" he asked, struggling to push it off.

Magdalena stepped toward him, pointed her assault rifle at his head, and fired on full automatic. The bullets became a veritable swarm of bees in front of his face, which pressed ever closer as they started to overwhelm the forcefield. Probably, she'd seen the specs on this forcefield, and knew how many bullets would overload it.

"Man, that's just *annoying*."

He hoped Lady Vengeance was having more luck.

~

Lady Vengeance and the Raven circled each other, blades raised. It might have seemed a poor match—the exhausted woman in black leather against the fresh man in enhanced power armor—but as they moved, darkness gathered around her, girding her with black steel. Fear armor.

"These aren't your powers," the Raven said. "You're using an image inducer."

"You mean that one?" Lady Vengeance nodded back to the inducer on the table, which was still projecting the blue forcefield around Liz.

"A different one," the Raven said. "One we didn't find."

"Maybe."

They met, exchanged half a dozen attacks and parries, and broke apart again. Now Lady Vengeance seemed taller, her eyes dripping black blood down her pale face.

"Having trouble reverse engineering it? That's because Stardust didn't invent it. Some crazy pulp science hero named Kara Sparx did. Apparently, she also created a functioning A.I. for her giant robot. Amazing, huh? All these things you *can't* do."

The Raven glared at her in reply. He'd never been one for banter—a weakness she was counting on.

They rushed each other again, and their blades sang. The Raven went on the offensive, hacking down at Lady Vengeance's defenses as she went down to one knee. Then Lady Vengeance caught his sword on her claw instead of the katana and countered with a slash that screeched across his power armor carapace. Vibroblade this wasn't, but she could penetrate his armor with a good, clean hit.

"I hit you with the dampener." The Raven sounded uneasy—making justifications to himself. "You can't be channeling my fear."

"Keep fighting—we'll see."

He was right, of course. The power dampener had done its work, and she was acting on pure adrenaline, not fear energy. Her increasingly demonic aspect was due not to the Raven's fear, but to the image induction looped into the wristwatch. It had been Stardust's idea: switch functions of the watch and inducer thingy-ma-jig so that Lady Vengeance could bluff her way through and still have the inducer. It was a feint, and one that might or might not pay off. She had to end the fight quickly, before the Raven got his bearings and realized what was going on.

Lady Vengeance attacked suddenly, and the Raven almost missed the parry. She locked his sword down low and raked at his face with her silvery claw. When she spoke again, it was not in her voice.

"*Is this not your fear, Antonio Desantes?*" she asked in Azazel's voice. "*That you will fail, and I will come forth, to destroy you and all you hold dear?*"

The Raven cringed, and Lady Vengeance pressed her advantage. She brought the sword down on his gauntlet blade with all of her strength, and the metal sheared off. The Raven retreated, and Lady Vengeance stepped forward to put her katana to his throat. She pressed him back against the wall.

Kill him, Azazel whispered. *Kill him, or you will lose.*

The sudden voice of the demon in Lady Vengeance's mind startled her, and she hesitated. "Give it up, Tony," she said. "You can't win. You can't defeat your worst fear."

Suddenly, the Raven's eyes were not scared but cold. "Can't I?"

Metal tore through leather, and sucking pain bloomed in her midsection. She looked down to where he had stabbed her in the stomach with the broken-off blade.

You lose, said Azazel in her mind. *Let me in.*

Strength suddenly left her, and she staggered back. The blade pulled free of her stomach, taking with it all her sense of balance. Her legs turned to jelly rolls that wouldn't support her weight, and she fell on her butt, holding her torn-open middle.

"I—I don't understand," she said. "Why … why aren't you afraid?"

Let me in! Azazel said with increasing urgency. *I have all your power. Give me yourself, and I will destroy him.*

The Raven drew away from the wall and ejected the bloody metal from his gauntlet. The shard clattered to the floor.

"My fear isn't that the demon will return," he said. "My fear is that I still love you."

Lady Vengeance stared up at him, completely at a loss. She felt like throwing up, and coughed blood onto her hand.

Let me in! Azazel demanded.

"And the only way to face that fear—" He drew his cape up, and Lady Vengeance saw two razor raven feathers slide into his hand. "—is to kill you."

Even so, he hesitated. They stood close together: lovers turned enemies, breathing hard and staring into each other's eyes. There was nothing more to be said. They had no hope of resolving this without a death.

LET ME IN!

"I'm sorry too." Lady Vengeance closed her eyes. "Take me, Azazel."

Then she started to change.

~

The machine gun bullets were getting remarkably close. They probably would have hit Stardust on the last run, had Magdalena not needed to stop and reload. He looked up at her now, through the swarm of angry lead, and realized he couldn't get the right angle to blast her. This was not looking good.

Then a shadow moved behind Magdalena and a wine bottle came down with shattering force on her head. She staggered a moment, looking confused, then slumped to the floor.

Liz emerged from behind her, broken wine bottle in hand. "Hi, honey," she said.

"Hi," he said. "Just a second—"

Havana appeared and slashed at Liz, but her vibroblade bounced off the forcefield. Stardust managed to line up his half-trapped gauntlet and blasted Havana through the balcony doors. She shrieked and fell off the Tower.

"Dispatch recovery drones to catch her," he said. "No sense making a mess."

"Right away, Jaccob," said the Computer. "*Stardust.*"

"Damn right. Now then: full power to Starbolts."

"Full power to—" The Computer said.

"Stand back, babe," he said to Liz, and fired. The satellite dish rose off Stardust and shot away into the kitchen, where the refrigerator caught it in a massive *crunch* of metal on metal. Liz winced, even as she helped Stardust up. "Sorry."

"Don't worry about it," she said, and pressed her lips to his.

"Weren't you doped up or something?" Stardust asked.

"The Raven administered an antidote at the same time," Liz said. "I think he did it on purpose, to limit the effect. So that I could escape, and you'd be free to—" Her face turned grave. "To do the right thing."

"The right thing—" Stardust looked toward the living room and the duel. He saw the Raven get the upper hand and stab Lady Vengeance in the stomach. "Wait!" he shouted, but the Raven raised his blades anyway.

Stardust jetted forward, grabbed the Raven's wrist, and hurled him away. The man crashed into the dining room table. In so doing, he destroyed the forcefield projector, and the blue air padding around Liz winked out of existence. They wrestled in the burned wreckage of his penthouse.

"No," the Raven was saying. "You idiot! You've doomed your city!"

"Shut up," Stardust said, and knocked the Raven down with a Starbolt.

A horrible, keening sound stabbed into his ears, and he almost fell over in his surprise. At first, he thought it must be Lady

Vengeance screaming in pain, but he saw the maniacal glee on her face and realized it was something else.

Laughter. Lady Vengeance was *laughing*, in a voice not her own.

"Idiot!" the Raven broadcast from the floor. "I could have stopped her. But now, it's too late."

"V?" Stardust asked. "What's going on?"

Lady Vengeance was changing: her teeth and ears lengthening, her body swelling with new muscle, her skin becoming as hard as chitin. Blackness seeped from her eyes and bat wings burst from her back. She fixed her maniac stare on him.

When she spoke, her voice was the rumble of thunder in the distance, the world cracking beneath his feet.

"*Lady Vengeance doesn't live here anymore,*" she said.

CHAPTER FIFTEEN

THE SUM OF ALL FEARS

The Raven clenched his fists to keep from passing out. That last Starbolt had hit him hard, and the world wavered around him. He focused on the pain—focused on what he had to do. He tried to fight the swell of fear that threatened to take him over. Whether it was fear for the world, himself, or *her*, he could not say.

The woman he knew as Vivienne Cain was gone, and only Azazel remained.

"*It's too late,*" the demon said. "*You are mine. This world is mine.*"

The words drew the Raven's attention to the living room. Stardust had fallen to his knees before Lady Vengeance, who traced designs with her claw over his faceplate. A huge smile split her face ear to ear.

The Raven was no match for the demon, and neither was Stardust. It had taken the entirety of Supergroup to defeat the possessed Lady Vengeance thirty years ago, and her powers had been new and untried then. How could the Raven even delay her, much less stop her? But he had to try.

If he died trying to stop this demon from entering the world, then so be it.

The Raven fired two razor-sharp feathers at her, but she interposed Stardust between them like a shield and deflected the feathers with his forcefield.

"*Hilarious, weak little man,*" she said. "*You could not kill this body before I took it. You think you can kill me now? Me!*"

As though under the demon's power, Stardust's arm came up and sent another Starbolt at the Raven. He managed to dodge and hurled another raven feather at the demon. She deflected that too, moving Stardust like a puppet. Then she set Stardust down, and he turned hesitantly toward the Raven.

"*I control a man's fears, I control the man,*" Azazel said. "*Kill him, my champion.*"

"No," Stardust said. "I ... won't—"

The skin on the Raven's heck and arms itched. He'd never seen the demon take over another hero like that—could that happen to him?

Lady Vengeance draped her arms around his neck and nuzzled against his ear. "Do it, Jaccob," she said in her own voice. "Do it for *me*."

"Ugh ... can't ... resist—"

Stardust raised his arms and sent two Starbolts searing across the living room. The Raven ducked to let the bolts shatter the wall behind him, then threw feathers and moved. His feathers shattered off the blue forcefield, and the Raven kept dodging Starbolts, any one of which could have crushed every bone in his body. If his blasts before had been set to nonlethal force, he showed no sign of holding back now.

"Kill him for me," Lady Vengeance said.

Stardust's boot-jets fired, and he shot across the room, gushing Starbolts. The Raven ducked and twisted and rolled, trying desperately to stay alive. A bolt winged his left arm, scorching through the power-enhancing exoskeleton there, and the arm went numb. A chunk of the floor ripped free and he stumbled, slamming his knee hard. In the second it took to free himself, the Raven couldn't dodge when Stardust circled around behind and blasted him into the floor with a Starbolt.

"You have to fight her, Jaccob Stevens," the Raven said. "You have to—"

"Can't—" Stardust blasted him again.

The Raven lay flat on his stomach, teeth chattering under the force. It couldn't have lasted more than five seconds, but it felt like it went on and on. The Starbolt drove him down through the cracking floorboards, and the pressure built and built. The Raven fought to breathe.

"Kill him!" Lady Vengeance cried. "Hit him aga—*ahh*!"

Across the room, Mrs. Stevens loomed out of the shadows and stabbed at Lady Vengeance with a broken wine bottle. "Let go of my husband, you bitch!"

The demon-possessed woman was so surprised that a jab got in and split her hand open. Lady Vengeance yanked her bloody hand back with a cry of pain.

"Uh." Stardust looked confused. "That wasn't—"

Then Lady Vengeance stepped forward and sucker-punched Liz in the face with her bloodied hand. "*Stupid whore!*" Azazel said. "*How dare you touch me!*"

"What ... ?" Stardust shook himself and looked around at the devastation as though waking from a dream. He saw his crumpled wife. "Liz!"

"Leave her, my Stardust," Lady Vengeance said. "Kill the Raven."

For a second, the Raven thought Stardust might throw off her control—seeing Liz so callously attacked like that—but then he nodded. "Yes, Mistress!"

Stardust blasted the Raven down hard enough that the floor broke beneath him. The Raven was briefly falling, weightless, and he slammed into the floor on the next level. Marjorie—who was just coming into work for the morning—took one look at the dusty, dented tech hero on the floor, and locked herself in the bathroom. The Raven heard her dialing the phone—911, presumably, though that would do more harm than good. He lay on the floor, coughing, and looked up at the hole in the ceiling. Stardust hovered over the gap, his gauntlets crackling.

"*Kill him!*" Azazel cried. "*Do it now!*"

"Yes, Mistress." Stardust aimed his gauntlets, and they hummed loudly.

The Raven knew he had only one option: one with a short window of opportunity. "Computer, Final Override, Charlie-Alpha-Romeo-Oscar."

Stardust's Computer responded immediately. "Welcome, Antonio Desantes. One last tryst, for old time's sake?"

"Oh hell no," Stardust said. "Not this bullshit again!"

The Raven engaged his boosters and leaped toward Stardust. A Starbolt zipped past his shoulder, and then he tackled Stardust up and into the air. Stardust tried to fend him off, but the Raven melted right through his forcefield and grabbed him by the neck.

His momentum knocked Stardust upside down, and they struggled in the air.

"Computer!" he shouted. "Engage boot-jets!"

They blasted downward.

~

"Oh, come on!" Stardust shouted.

His boot-jets fired, and they jetted down into Starcom Tower. With the Jaccobean forcefield surrounding them both, they blasted faster and faster through floor after floor. As they went, they wrestled in the air, kicking and punching and shoving at one another. The Raven was clearly a better hand-to-hand fighter, but Stardust thought his attacks and blocks were sluggish—tired. The Raven switched to fighting dirty: gouges, low-blows, and hidden blades that popped from his gauntlets and boots. Most of it did nothing to Stardust through his heavy armor, of course, but it kept him from focusing on their course.

They crashed through into the lobby of the first floor, which looked like a set from a high-caliber action movie, and slammed headfirst into the stone with a thunderous roar. This, Stardust wasn't powerful enough to drive through, so they bounced off, rolled, and lay gasping on the concrete floor. The forcefield had absorbed most of the impact, and now they lay in a crater several feet deep.

Stardust sat up and shook his head. "Wow, what hit m—"

The Raven lunged across and wrestled Stardust to the floor. "Listen," he said. "Listen to me! The demon has control of her. You have to—" He opened his faceplate and coughed blood onto the floor. "You have to stop her."

Stardust blinked at him. "But—"

"Listen to me!" the Raven insisted. "I can't do it. I tried, but now I'm too weak. You need to do it." He thrust his face into Stardust's own, such that their noses almost touched. "*You* have to kill her."

"But I can't," Stardust said. "I can't just kill her. I—"

"If you won't do it to protect yourself, do it to protect your city—your world. Protect your *wife*, dammit! Elizabeth could be dying up there right now."

Stardust drew in a sharp breath. "You—I cannot disobey my mistress."

"Then we are all dead," the Raven said, his words soft.

Stardust put his hands under the Raven's armpits and activated his boot-jets. They shot back up toward the penthouse, where Lady Vengeance was waiting. She seemed darker and more powerful than before, with wings spreading out around her. A struggling Liz hung from her clawed hand. "*How sweet—you've brought me my offering.*"

Stardust trembled, his hands working over and over. The Raven was looking at him—one last entreaty.

The time was now.

Stardust's hands tightened into fists. "No."

Lady Vengeance raised her eyebrows. "*No?*"

He fired a Starbolt to knock the demon that was Lady Vengeance against the opposite wall. She staggered back, then looked up at him, shocked. "*How dare you. You think I fear a tiny man with a tiny mind? You are nothing.*"

"I'm Stardust, dammit!" He caught her with a Starbolt that made her whole body shudder under the force.

Lady Vengeance fell to one knee, surrounded by the ashen circle his blast had burned into the carpet. One of her arms, seemingly separate from her body, rose and gestured at Stardust, who stumbled back, coughing. She was still fighting: fighting the demon even as it fought all of them.

"Please, Vivienne!" Liz shouted. "I know you're in there!"

Lady Vengeance brought her hands up to her temples. "Mmhh, I—I—"

Stardust hit her again, and she screamed, seemingly hurt for the first time. She sank back against the wall, supporting herself by the thinnest shred of strength. When she looked up again, it was with her own eyes. She seemed dizzy.

"J-Jaccob? Goddammit, I—I let him in and now I can't get him out!" She screamed and grasped her head. "There's no choice left. You have to kill me."

"Wait, what?" Stardust's heart raced. "Kill you? I can't—"

"Do it!" Lady Vengeance begged. "Do it now, before he comes back!"

"I'm not a killer. I can't just—"

Lady Vengeance grabbed and held his gauntleted hand to her face. He held his hand closed, refusing to open it to reveal his Starblaster.

"Fuck you!" she roared. "Stop being a pussy and just do it!"

"No," Stardust said. "There has to be another way to stop this."

"There really isn't." Lady Vengeance stared up at him with her dark eyes that were her own and not those of any demon. "If I'm going to die, I'll die as myself."

This was it, then—the moment of truth. Stardust looked to Liz, who regarded him with a devastated expression, then the Raven, who nodded once. He turned back to Lady Vengeance, and his hand opened. His gauntlet hummed with a rising charge.

"Thank God." She smiled blissfully. "It's over."

Stardust shut his eyes and fired.

~

It took only a second. She was standing there—beautiful in her acceptance—and then the blast went through her head. She drew up taut, standing completely straight. Then her body collapsed with what sounded to the Raven like a relieved sigh.

Darkness fell around the Raven, and he found only sadness waiting.

EPILOGUE

THE MORNING AFTER

When light filtered back in through the darkness, Antonio Desantes became aware of a warm softness that suffused him. He wondered for a few seconds if he was dead, but he'd been in enough hospitals to recognize the feeling.

He opened his eyes, which focused to show him an intensive care unit. He was mostly naked—stripped to a hospital gown and deprived of his power armor—but aside from a general numbness, he felt all right.

A nurse in blue scrubs was taking his vitals, but Antonio caught the man's hand. "Speak," he said. "Where am I? How did I get here?"

"Calm down, sir," said the nurse. "You're at Starcom's private trauma ward. You were in need of serious medical attention—"

"I'm fine," Antonio said. "Answer my question."

"That's enough, Henry." Liz Stevens put her hand on the nurse's shoulder. "Why don't you report to the doctor?"

"Sure boss." The nurse went away, casting anxious looks back over his shoulder.

Liz stood next to Antonio's bed, an ugly bruise across her face. She wore a cast over her hand, though Antonio didn't remember her hurting her hand in the fight. His Ravens were there too: Havana, her arm in a sling and bandages across her face, looked at him forlornly, while Magdalena studied the patterns in the linoleum and held an ice pack to the back of her head. Lastly, Jaccob Stevens leaned against the wall and stared out the window, arms crossed. He pointedly did not look at Antonio.

"What happened?" he asked. "Is she—?"

The look on Liz's face was enough to answer Antonio's question. He nodded.

It was over, then. Not that Antonio felt in the least bit relieved.

"You haven't turned any of us in to the authorities," he said. "Thank you for that."

"You never meant to hurt *us*." Liz shook her head. "You can even have your suit back. Though you should expect a bill for damages—a big one."

"Valhalla honors its debts." Antonio addressed his words primarily to Jaccob, though the man didn't look at him. "You were a worthy adversary, one I would much prefer to have as an ally. One day, when all this has faded behind us, we should talk."

Jaccob drummed his fingers on his arms and said nothing.

Antonio had expected as much. He turned to Liz. "We will go now. No doubt you have work to do, as do we." He detached himself from the machines and got up despite protesting aches. H and M rose on cue.

"That's it?" Jaccob asked from the window.

Antonio froze in the doorway.

"Honey," Liz said. "You said—"

"I said I wasn't going to say anything, but I have to." Jaccob turned to Antonio. "A woman is dead, and that's it? You're not going to say anything about her?"

"What is there to say?"

"How you feel about it?" Jaccob said. "Obviously you had something, and obviously you've hated her for a long time. Don't you feel—I don't know, *sorry* about her death? Angry? Sad? Anything?"

From his tight expression to his clenched fists to his shivering leg muscles, everything about Jaccob Stevens spoke of barely restrained anger.

"This is the first time you've killed someone, yes?" Antonio asked.

Jaccob snapped. Unarmored—just a man against a trained warrior—he lunged across the room with a cry. Not that Antonio would have resisted.

Liz restrained Jaccob, and while he struggled free, he kept glaring at Antonio. "*You* did this. If you hadn't hounded her into a corner, this never would have happened. Remember that."

"It gets easier," Antonio said. "It shouldn't, but it does."

Jaccob stepped toward him again, but Liz interposed herself and raised her hands in silent supplication. Antonio found himself pondering her bandaged hand. When had that happened? Maybe ...

"Just get out, Raven." Jaccob narrowed his eyes. "Keep your money and your sympathy. Just get out of my damn city."

Antonio nodded, and he and his Ravens left.

~

The sound of jets atop Starcom Tower signaled the Raven's departure, along with his minions. Jaccob knew they would not return to Cobalt City—at least not for some time. And if they did, well, Jaccob had had more than enough time to analyze the Raven's tech while he lay unconscious, and his mind had already cooked up half a dozen traps to set for him. The next time the Raven decided to trespass on Jaccob's turf, he would find himself very unwelcome.

"Well," he said. "You think he bought it?"

The image of Liz wavered. Her pretty blonde hair and perfect tan became raven-black hair and pale skin, and her light eyes became so deep blue they were almost purple. The bruise on her face disappeared and she blew out a relaxed sigh. "You'd think he'd catch on," Vivienne said as she set the image inducer watch on the counter. "That's some tech. Couldn't have done better myself, and I have *magic*."

"Just a program I threw together at the last minute—I'm glad it worked," Jaccob said. "You're the one who convinced him you'd gone all devil—you half-convinced me, too. You ever considered being an actress?"

"Tried that once—thanks but no thanks," she said. "You weren't so bad yourself."

"Yeah? I thought I was laying it on pretty thick." Jaccob raised his arms in an imitation of a zombie. "Can't ... resist ... must obey ... my mistress!"

"I know, right? Speaking of mistresses who must be obeyed, how's Liz?"

"Nursing a sprained jaw and pretty pissed," Jaccob said. "I guess it looked real this way, but I wish we could have told her about the plan to fake your death before."

"My hand does too." Vivienne touched her bandaged hand and winced. "Your wife swings a wicked wine bottle."

"You can say that again. Lucky she didn't cut any tendons. It'll scar, though."

"I'll add it to the collection of liquor-related injuries."

"Of course you have a list like that." Jaccob picked up the image inducer watch. "You want to take this with you? Just in case the Raven figures it out?"

"Oh, I plan to be far, far away before he figures out I'm still breathing," Vivienne said. "I'm thinking Bora Bora."

Jaccob nodded. "So ... when you used the image inducer, he thought Azazel had taken over. But then, when he had you on the ropes, he didn't kill you. Why not?"

Vivienne returned an enigmatic smile. "You'd be surprised how often what we most fear is what we think we want."

"You know—" Jaccob thought of the previous week, and his fantasies about leaving his family and jetting off into the sunset to be Stardust. "Actually, I wouldn't."

"No, I suppose you wouldn't." Vivienne nodded. "We improvised well. The Raven could have killed me, but he didn't. And I—" She trailed off and sighed.

"I am so glad I don't have your relationship problems."

"Yeah, you are," Vivienne said. "But you need to buy your wife some flowers or an island or something. She really saved your butt there. I came pretty close."

"Oh, you wouldn't have unleashed the devil with your fear powers and killed everyone in Cobalt City. Right? V?" Jaccob cleared his throat nervously.

Lady Vengeance gave him a wry smile, a friendly kiss on the cheek, and left.

"Right?"

ABOUT THE AUTHOR

Erik Scott de Bie is a 30-something speculative fiction author and game designer.

He has published ten novels to date, including novels in the storied Forgotten Realms, his World of Ruin epic fantasy setting (the fourth of which, *Scourge of the Broken World*, is due out in 2019), as well as stand-alone novels for Broken Eye Books (*Scourge of the Realm*) and the horror novel *Blind Justice*.

His short work has appeared in numerous anthologies and online, and he is the author of the multimedia superhero project, *Justice/Vengeance* (including fiction, spoken word, and comics).

In his work as a game designer, he has contributed to products from such companies as Wizards of the Coast and Privateer Press, and he was the lead creative consultant on *Red Aegis* from Vorpal Games.

He lives in Seattle with his wife, cats, and dog. Learn more at erikscottdebie.com.

ABOUT THE COVER ARTIST

With a deep love in the fantastic, Lori Krell creates pen, pencil, and digital art for novels, game books, and more. A lifetime spent reading and gaming in fantasy, science fiction, and comic book worlds has influenced her work. She has published a number of works including detailed world maps, personalized character portraits, action scenes of characters in their worlds, and covers. Check out her portfolio at lorikrell.myportfolio.com.

www.ingramcontent.com/pod-product-compliance
Lightning Source LLC
Chambersburg PA
CBHW072238190626
46809CB00018B/2843

* 9 7 8 1 9 4 8 2 8 0 1 0 5 *